SWEET TEA B&B

RACHEL HANNA

CHAPTER 1

"Three-hundred and sixty five days. That's the number of days in one year. Sometimes, it seems so long, especially when the year has gone like this one. Watching cancer ravage my Momma, who lived twenty thousand seventy-four days, one day shy of her fifty-fifth birthday, has been the hardest thing I've ever done.

To some, those thousands of days may seem like a long time. To me, it all seemed awfully short. She didn't live enough days to see me meet the man of my dreams. To see me walk down the aisle at my wedding. To see me raise my own children. She didn't live long enough to play with her future grandkids. So much life will be missed.

But she did live long enough to know I loved her, that we all loved her. She knew that I was happy and that I would take care of her beloved Sweet Tea B&B.

She was the heart of the B&B, and her spirit and

soul will be missed, but I know my Momma will always be here with me. My tears may soak my pillow every night for the rest of my life, but I know where my Momma is, and I feel so thankful to have been her daughter. What a blessing from God. Thank you."

As Mia stepped away from the pulpit, where she stood in front of a packed crowd of people in her mother's home church, she let out the breath she'd been holding for days. Public speaking wasn't her forte, especially when she was so entrenched in grief.

When the service wrapped up, she found herself surrounded by well-meaning friends, each of them hugging her tightly and telling her time healed all wounds. She'd always hated that saying. After losing her dog of twelve years when she was twenty years old, she knew that saying was a bunch of crap. She still missed Ranger even though she was thirty-four years old.

"Oh, honey, I'm going to miss your sweet Momma," Olivia Winegarden said. She'd been a longtime customer of the B&B, always showing up around Thanksgiving to spend time soaking in the beauty of the north Georgia mountains.

"Thank you, Miss Livy. I hope you'll still come stay at the B&B."

"Of course, my dear," the older woman said. "I sure hope your Momma left her peach cobbler recipe, though. I've come to look forward to that every time I visit."

Mia smiled. "I have it in a safe place, trust me."

As everyone filed out of the church, Mia felt the grief start to wash over her again. It was hard having no family to turn to. Sure, she had friends and customers, but her mother was the only one who shared her blood.

Mia's mother, Charlene, had only been twenty years old when she'd given birth to her, yet Mia had never lacked for anything. One day, she hoped to be half the mother Charlene was. She'd always been involved in Mia's school, volunteering as room mother and chaperoning field trips. Working three jobs for most of Mia's formative years, Charlene had seemed like a pillar of strength, never showing the inevitable fear she must have felt trying to raise a child on her own for so many years.

They'd grown up together, really, with Mia watching her mother date. Finally, when Mia was ten, Charlene had married Bobby, a nice enough guy who worked as an electrician. They'd gotten along well, and he had always treated her mother well. They bought their first house together, and Charlene started a business as a caterer.

She was an amazing cook, always coming up with new and innovative recipes, especially for such a rural area. Charlene was sought after, always providing food for parties, weddings and other events in the area. As time went on, she and Bobby bought what would become Sweet Tea B&B, fulfilling Charlene's dream of owning a bed and breakfast in the foothills of the Blue Ridge Mountains.

When Bobby keeled over with a massive heart attack, Mia was eighteen years old. Instead of leaving for college, like she'd planned, she'd stepped in to help her mother run the B&B. It was supposed to be for a year, just until things got up and running again after Bobby's death and Charlene's grieving period. But, she'd never left and would continue to run the B&B now that her mother had passed away.

True, it wasn't her lifelong dream at first, but she'd grown to love the place and the people who came through the large home over the years. Couples on their honeymoons, women starting over, families on vacation, friends making memories. Every person who stayed there had a story, and Mia loved to hear them all.

Her mother had often said that she had one of those faces that people saw and immediately wanted to tell their life story to, and that was pretty accurate. Mia loved to sit and hear the stories that her customers brought with them from around the country. Some stories of heartache, others of triumph. She often felt trapped a bit in her small part of the world, holding down the fort at the Sweet Tea B&B. Not that she didn't love it, but sometimes there was a void.

The void of not having love in her life was the biggest one. It was times like this that she wished she had a man to put his arms around her and tell her everything was going to be okay. That he would back her up. That she wasn't alone. Yet, she was alone, literally and figuratively.

As she stood in the middle of the little Southern Baptist church, complete with wooden pews and musty old hymnals, she felt more alone in the world than she ever had.

~

KATE STOOD in the middle of the large banquet hall. The Seymour wedding reception was one of the biggest parties she'd ever planned, and she was currently sweating bullets over the whole thing. Tomorrow night would either be the biggest moment in her career, or she'd been run out of town by angry Seymours carrying pitchforks and chanting "death to Kate Miller!"

Or maybe that was just a bit dramatic.

At thirty-seven years old, this party planning company was her second act. After her divorce five years ago, she felt adrift in her life. Not knowing what to do after being a stay at home mother for most of her married life, she was left a single mother with no education or experience. Starting her own business had been both a dream and a terrifying nightmare that sometimes woke her up out of a dead sleep, sweat dripping down her face.

"Kate?"

She turned to see Holly Jameson, the bride to be, standing behind her. Holly was the epitome of a young woman who came from a wealthy Rhode

Island family. Perfect, long blonde hair swept up into a messy top knot that was actually made to look messy but probably took an hour to do. Perfect makeup with highlights and lowlights painted on like a piece of artwork. Perfect clothing from only the most expensive stores in town. And she was perfectly awful to work for, as if being demanding and rude seemed to be hobbies of hers.

"Hi, Holly. I didn't know you were here yet."

She looked down at her Apple Watch and then wrinkled her nose a bit. "I'm always early. Punctuality is one of the cornerstones of who I am."

Kate stared at her for a moment, silently trying to figure out who would want to be married to her for the rest of their life. She cleared her throat. "Right. What can I do for you?"

She scrunched her nose again, something she would inevitably get filled in when wrinkles started showing up in a few more years. "I have to say, I'm just not overwhelmed with these decorations. I expected the flowers to be… more…"

"More what?"

"Floral."

Kate felt an urge to throat punch someone for the first time in her life.

"Floral? But, aren't flowers inherently floral?"

"One would think. I feel we need some pops of color. After all, this is *my* wedding. It has to be perfect!"

Kate thought back to her own wedding to Brandon all those years ago. They were really just kids themselves when they got married, and it didn't go well from the start. Having their daughter, Evie, was the glue that held them together for so many years. Without her, they would've divorced early on. They stayed together until she was ten, and then Kate just couldn't take it anymore.

Now fifteen years old, Evie was a handful. The school was constantly calling, complaining about her skipping school, acting out and just generally being a bad kid. Kate often wondered where she'd gone wrong in raising her daughter. She'd had a wonderful single mother, so she tried to model her late mother's strong spirit. Most of the time, she just wanted to lock herself in her walk-in closet and cry. She had no idea what to do with her daughter.

Brandon was in and out of Evie's life, but mostly out. He'd been good in the first couple of years, taking her on daddy daughter dates every other weekend and even showing up at her soccer games. Then, he met Kara and moved to Mexico to start a new family with her. Evie definitely felt abandoned, but she wouldn't voice it. She acted out instead.

"Hello?" Holly said, waving her fake fingernail laden hand in front of Kate's face.

"Oh, sorry. I zoned out there for a moment."

"Please call the florist and work this out. We only have a few hours before we exchange our vows, and this place is not ready. Honestly, Kate, I hired you based on the recommendation of my hair stylist, but I'm starting to wonder if you're up to this job."

Her blood was boiling. As much as she wanted to

be successful in the wealthier circles in town, the people she had to deal with were some of the worst. She wanted to run screaming out of the building, but instead she pasted on a fake smile.

"Of course, Holly. Now that I know you need pops of color, I'll drive to the florist myself and hand choose what we need. No worries. When you walk into this room tonight, it will be the reception of your dreams. Okay?"

She jutted out her chin and crossed her arms. "I certainly hope so." With that, she turned to walk away. Kate started to raise her arm up to give her a special hand signal, but quickly thought better of it. Holly suddenly turned back around. "Oh, and please make sure the food gets here on time, but not too early. I don't want the stuffed mushrooms to be cold and mushy."

Holly walked out of the hall, her heels clicking across the hardwood floor. As Kate looked around at her handiwork, she was proud of what she'd done, but apparently her client didn't feel the same.

～

Mia stood in the middle of the kitchen, her mother's recipe cards spread across the island. Today, she was making her hash brown casserole, complete with real chunks of bacon. Guests always loved that for breakfast, so she'd gotten up early to make it since she had several new guests coming that morning.

She ran her finger across her mother's beautiful handwriting, her eyes welling with tears. It had only been a couple of weeks since Charlene had passed away, but to Mia everyday felt like a long, slow slog up a hill of quicksand. She missed her mother with every fiber of her being.

Not all kids had grown up with such a great mother, but Mia felt she'd been blessed. Charlene had experienced a rough upbringing herself, something she didn't talk about much. But her inner strength in raising Mia had always been apparent. At thirty-four years old, Mia hadn't found Mr. Right, so she'd never been married or had kids. Alone in the world now, she felt like an orphan and wished she had someone to turn to in times like this.

Friends and guests were great, and she adored them. But she wanted someone who shared her blood. Her genes. Her very life force. And now that her mother was gone, she would never have that. She would spend the rest of her life as the only one in her line of Carters. She sighed and tried to pull herself out of the funk she was in.

"Morning, Mia," Dr. Allen said as he walked into the kitchen. He came to stay at the B&B with his wife a few times a year. They lived in Atlanta, so not very far away, but they loved the seclusion and atmosphere around the bed and breakfast.

"Good morning. I'm getting a bit of a late start today, but I'm making my Momma's hashbrown casserole. I've already made some cheese grits if you'd like some. They're in the pot over there. The biscuits are still cooking, but we've got some sawmill gravy in the other pot."

He smiled. "No hurry, sweetie. I know it's hard to run this place without Charlene. We're so going to miss her. She was so young." Dr. Allen was in his eighties, but still very spry and active. He loved playing tennis at his club back in the city. Having retired from being a general practitioner for decades, he and his wife did a lot of traveling now.

"Yes, she was. It's not fair, is it?" Mia took a break from stirring the ingredients together and pulled her thick, wavy blond hair back into a ponytail. At barely five feet tall, she had to stand on a small stool just to get things out of the cabinet. Her mother hadn't been quite as short at five foot three. Amazing how those three inches made such a difference in what she could reach.

"I've seen a lot of unfairness in life in my time as a physician. But, we know where she is, don't we?"

"Of course. And she'll always be my angel. But still…"

"Still what?"

"Oh nothing. I'm just being nostalgic."

"What do you mean?"

She smiled. "I'm a little lonely with no family left."

"None? What about cousins?"

"No one that I know of. Momma was an only child, and her parents died before I was born."

"Well, that's terrible, sweetie. Say, you know, I've

heard about these DNA tests you can do to find extended family. Have you done one?"

"No, I haven't. I mean, would distant cousins even want to have contact?"

"Well, I reckon they might if they're putting their DNA out there."

Mia thought for a moment. "You might be onto something there, Dr. Allen. I might just give that a shot. Who knows? Maybe I have a famous or wealthy relative who will add me to their will one day," she said, with a laugh.

"Anything's possible!"

~

KATE SAT on the doctor's table, her legs touching the floor easily. Most women had legs that dangled cutely off the edge of the table. Her legs were long, easily plopping onto the ground in a non-feminine way.

She'd always hated her height. At five foot ten, she was as tall as or taller than most of the men she'd met. Even her ex husband was shorter than her.

Being tall had not only made her stick out in school, but even in her own family. Her mother was average height, and her father was too, although she didn't like to think about him. After her parents divorce when she was in fourth grade, her father had left the picture and started a whole new family across the country. She hadn't spoken to him in years. She'd tried to reach out a few times over the years, but he finally admitted to her that he didn't want contact. He wanted his new family, and that was that.

Nobody knew where she got her unusual height. Her mother once said it must've been a distant relative, but Kate didn't know much about her extended family tree. She'd often thought about getting one of those DNA test kits she saw online, but never really got excited enough to actually pay for one.

"I just don't get it. My asthma has been under control since I was a kid," she said to her doctor.

"Sometimes stress can aggravate it. Have you been under stress lately?" Dr. Alvarez asked.

Kate laughed out loud. "Nah. I just have an out of control teenage daughter and a fledgling business. No big deal."

The doctor smiled slightly. "Sounds like you need some support, Kate. Have you thought about…"

"What? Counseling? No thanks. I've had my daughter in counseling for years, and a lot of good it's done."

"Well, what about family? Anyone who can help, maybe take the strain off of you a bit?"

Kate sighed. "Look, doc, I don't really have access to that sort of thing. I have a couple of pretty decent friends, but that's about it. My mother passed away when I was twenty, Evie's father is absent and I have no siblings."

"I'm sorry to hear that. You know, it's also possible that your asthma has a genetic component.

Might be good to get that checked out for your daughter's sake."

"How do I do that?"

"You can get an online DNA test. Might also help you find some relatives you didn't know you had." She smiled as she handed Kate a piece of paper. "This is the company I recommend. Turnaround is a few weeks, though, so be prepared for a wait."

"I do know that I'm a mix of German and Austrian," she said, looking down at the paper.

"Hmmm," the doctor said, tilting her head.

"What?"

"Well, it's just that I see a lot of people, and I've seen a lot of DNA results. I wouldn't have pegged you for German or Austrian. More like Irish and English."

"Really? Well, maybe you'll be surprised when I bring my results in next time," she said with a chuckle.

"Maybe so."

CHAPTER 2

*M*ia sat at the breakfast bar, her laptop open. Paying bills always made her antsy. Would she have enough money this month to cover everything? It had been awfully close last month. The more she had to handle the entire business alone, the more she appreciated what her mother had been able to accomplish for all those years. She made it seem easy, and Mia was starting to feel like a bit of a failure.

Her biggest fear now was destroying everything her mother had built. She tried to keep positive, but it was hard, especially at night. Since breaking up with her last boyfriend, Evan, a year ago, she'd missed having a shoulder to cry on when times were hard. Evan wanted to travel, and she couldn't. She wasn't about to leave her mother behind when she was so sick, and Evan knew she'd take over the business after her mother died, so he broke it off saying he needed more.

Well, she needed more too. More time with her mother. More money to pay the bills. More support. Or *any* support really.

Even her friends had started to steer clear of her, probably getting tired of hearing her talk about missing her mother. But she couldn't help it. Grief was the hardest thing she'd ever experienced, and it didn't feel like it was getting any better.

Sure, she didn't cry all day long now. It had been weeks since her mother passed away. But she cried at the oddest times, like when she smelled her mother's bread cooking in the oven. Or when she accidentally broke one of her mother's favorite coffee mugs. It was pink with a fluffy white kitten on it. She sat on the floor that morning with a tube of glue and tears running down her face.

It was hard doing life alone.

Her mother had been her best friend, although she'd never really realized that until it was too late. Kids, especially girls, tend to take their mothers for granted, and she'd been guilty of that. She often wondered if her mother really knew how much she loved her, how much she appreciated all of the things she'd done for her. The times she'd taken care of her when she was sick. The times she'd scraped to get by, trying to make ends meet, and still found a way to buy that special gift at Christmas. The times she'd let Mia cry on her shoulder over boys whose names she couldn't even remember now.

"Ugh," she said to herself as she stared at the screen. Thankfully, all of her guests were asleep for the night, so she had some time to herself. Running a B&B was exhausting work, but she loved it. It made her feel close to her mother.

Her email dinged, and she welcomed the opportunity to click away from one of the many billing tabs she had open. It was the DNA company where she'd sent her sample a few weeks back. She followed the prompts to see her results.

"Well, let's see," she said to herself. "I'm mostly Irish. No surprise there…"

As she continued clicking around, she learned about different genetic traits she had, possible diseases she could contract - what a happy thought - and where her ancestors had originally come from.

The site also had a way to connect with relatives. She clicked on it and immediately saw some matches. Mostly, they were very distant cousins, people who probably wouldn't relish the idea of a perfect stranger contacting them and asking if she could come to the next family reunion or eat Christmas dinner with them.

Just as she was about to click away and go back to crying over the bills, she noticed another family connection. This one didn't say cousin. It said… sister?

Only she didn't have a sister. No siblings at all. Her mother was only twenty when she had her, after all. Basically just a baby herself.

Mia had never been more confused in her life, but she was determined to get to the bottom of this. And she knew just who could help her.

~

KATE WAS LIVID. She stood in the principal's office for the umpteenth time, shaking her head as she looked at her daughter. Evie was sitting in the chair, slumped down with her arms crossed. Kate had gotten used to the scowl on her face, but today it was particularly irritating, not to mention embarrassing.

"Mr. Hayes, I'm so sorry. Again. I just don't know what to do with her right now. Evie, don't you have something to say for your behavior?"

Evie glared up at both of them standing over her. "Nope."

"Evie!" Kate scolded, although it rarely worked.

"Look, it wasn't even a big deal," she said, rolling her eyes.

"Miss Miller, I can assure you that putting gum in another student's hair is a big deal. The school nurse had to cut it out, and Sherri lost a few inches of her hair."

Evie stifled a laugh. "She deserves it. Do you know what a skank Sherri is? She's slept with half the football team!"

"Evie Miller, shut your mouth!" Kate said, wanting to tackle her daughter and tape her mouth shut.

"Whatever," she said, rolling her eyes again. That was her go-to move, mainly because she knew Kate hated it.

"Evelyn," the principal said to his secretary, who

was standing near the door, "please take Miss Miller to the other room so I can speak with her mother."

Evie sighed and followed Evelyn to the other room, the door slamming shut behind them. Kate knew this wasn't good.

"Please, have a seat." He pointed to a chair across from his desk and then took his place across from her, interlacing his fingers together in front of him.

"You're kicking her out, aren't you?"

He smiled sadly. "I have no choice, Kate. We've given her more chances than any other student who has done these sorts of things. The only reason I've given her so much latitude is because I know you. You threw a wonderful anniversary party for Marilyn and myself last year. But, I can't keep covering for her. She's ratcheting her behavior up."

Kate took in a deep breath and blew it out. "What am I going to do with this kid?"

"I don't know. Maybe enroll her in the alternative high school?"

"Alternative high school?"

"They cater to kids with behavior problems, pregnant students, and so on."

Kate didn't want her daughter there. She wanted her to thrive in a regular high school, but how? She couldn't seem to make her understand that she was throwing her future away for nothing.

"Is she in counseling?"

"She was, but honestly we stopped going because sometimes she'd just sit there and not speak."

"Maybe a retreat or wilderness experience?"

"I don't know. Maybe. I have to think this through."

"I'm really sorry, Kate. Your daughter is obviously tormented by something in her mind. But the public school isn't the place to work those things out. I have to protect the other students here. I hope you understand."

She did. She wished she could defend her daughter, but there was no defense.

"I'll take her to clean out her locker, and then we'll go." She stood up and shook his hand. "Thanks for trying, Dan."

"Good luck. I hope it all works out."

As she quietly left the room and collected her daughter, she wondered what in the world she was going to do now.

∽

MIA TAPPED her foot nervously as she waited for Carl to enter the room. He had been her mother's attorney for as long as she could remember, handling all sorts of issues for the B&B. He had also handled her estate when she passed away, reading her will to Mia and a couple of close friends who she'd left some of her personal possessions to.

"Sorry to keep you waiting, Mia. I had a client meeting run a little long." He sat down behind his old, wooden desk - something from the seventies, no doubt - and looked at her. His balding head reflected the fluorescent lights above, and his white button up shirt was pulling so hard on the buttons that she feared one might pop off and blind her.

"No problem."

"So, what brings you here today, my dear?"

"I found out some shocking information, and I want to know if Momma ever said anything to you."

"Alrighty, what is it?"

Mia pulled a paper out of her bag showing the DNA results. She slid it across his desk and waited.

"What is this?"

"I did one of those online DNA tests, you know, just looking for information on where my family originated. They have this feature where you can find extended family members who have also done these DNA tests. Look at this one," she said, pointing at a line on the paper.

"Sister." He said it so matter of factly, no question mark at the end.

"Why don't you seem surprised?"

Carl leaned back against his creaky, leather chair and took off this glasses, rubbing between his eyes. "Well, I never thought this day would come."

"What are you talking about?"

He stood up and walked over to his file cabinet, an old wooden one you normally didn't see anymore. He pulled out a drawer and dug out a box in the back. She recognized it. It was one of her mother's old jewelry boxes, a simple handmade oak one that her grandfather had made for her when she was a girl. Mia hadn't realized it was missing until now.

"Is that my Momma's?"

He sat back down and put his hands on top of it. "Yes, it is."

"I don't understand what's going on."

"Many years ago, your mother came to me and told me that she had another daughter, about three years older than you. She wanted to find her, but she didn't really have the means for hiring a private investigator or anything."

"You must be mistaken, Carl. Momma would've told me I had a sister. I always wanted a sibling. I complained about it all the time," she said, smiling.

"I know this is hard, sweetie, but you do have a sister. And now it's right here in black and white."

She stared at him and then back down at the paper. "Why would she do this? Why didn't she tell me? Why did she give her away? I don't understand any of this." With a history of anxiety and panic attacks, Mia did her best to take long, deep breaths. The last thing she needed was a mental breakdown right in the middle of Carl's office.

"She was just a kid herself, Mia. At seventeen years old, she wasn't able to take care of a child. I suppose she did what she thought was best for the baby."

"Momma couldn't have given a baby away. She loved being a mother. I don't know what to think."

Carl cleared his throat. "There's something else, Mia."

"There's more? I don't know if I can take any more."

He opened the box and pulled out an envelope. "Your mother asked me to keep this for her in the event that her daughter ever found you. She wanted me to read it to the both of you. Together."

"What? Why?"

"I don't know, darlin'. I'm just trying to follow her wishes. But, I think you need to contact your sister and ask her to come here. Maybe it will give you some closure?"

"Closure? I have more questions than answers right now. I don't expect closure is coming any time soon."

"I know this all comes as a shock, but think of it this way. You have a sister now. Isn't that good news?"

Mia thought for a moment. "Well, I guess that all depends on what this sister of mine is like, doesn't it?"

～

KATE STOOD with her arms crossed in front of her daughter. She wanted to say she'd never been this mad before, but that would be a lie. She'd been this angry at her daughter a number of times recently.

"Evie, what am I going to do with you?"

"Send me on a nice long vacation?"

"This isn't funny!"

"Oh, come on, Mom. Teenagers act out all the time. This isn't a big deal," she groaned as she leaned her head back, her long, dark hair splaying over the back of the chair.

Kate sighed and sat down on the ottoman. "Evie, what is bothering you so much that you need to do these things? I want to help you."

She sat up and glared at her mother. "Don't treat me like I'm crazy. I'm just being a teenager."

"I didn't say you were crazy, Ev. I don't even believe that. But, you're throwing away your future doing these stupid things. Something is obviously upsetting you, and I'm your mother…"

"Stop it! Please!" Evie said, standing up and stomping toward her room. A few moments later, Kate heard her slam the door.

She shuddered when she thought about her daughter's future. What kind of life would she have if she kept behaving this way? The what ifs kept her up many nights.

Just a couple of years ago, they had a different relationship filled with shopping trips, mother daughter dates and the occasional pedicure. Now, they butted heads constantly, and Kate couldn't find one thing to praise about her daughter. All she did was discipline her, and she hated it.

She missed the days when Evie was a little girl, only interested in unicorns and baby dolls. Now, she played horrendous music so loud in her room that the downstairs neighbors kept calling the landlord of their apartment building and complaining.

There were times she thought about calling Brandon, her ex-husband, and begging him to take her, but she knew that wasn't the answer. Evie hadn't talked to her father in years, and Brandon seemed to have no interest in a relationship with her. It was all just so sad.

Kate made herself a cup of coffee and sat down on the sofa. Just as she laid her head back and closed her eyes for a moment of peace, her phone buzzed in her jean pocket. She lifted her hips in the air and dug it out. The number didn't look familiar, so she sent it to voicemail and leaned her head back again. Moments later, her phone buzzed again. Same number. Worried that it was an emergency of some kind, she finally answered.

"Hello?"

"Is this Kate Miller?"

"Yes, it is. Who is this?"

"My name is Carl Stowers. I live in Carter's Hollow Georgia."

"Carter's Hollow? That's the name of a real place?" Kate didn't like to think of herself as uppity, but this man's thick Southern accent and podunk town name didn't make her take him too seriously.

"Yes, ma'am, it surely is."

"And you're calling me because?"

"Well, I don't exactly know how to put this, Miss Miller. I guess I should just say it. Your birthmother has passed away, and she left you something. I was hoping you could come to my office so we can chat?"

Kate sat there frozen. Her birthmother? She wasn't adopted. Her mother died when she was twenty years old, and her father hadn't been around since she was a kid.

"Sir, you must have me confused with another Kate Miller because I'm not adopted."

He cleared his throat. "Oh dear. I assumed you knew."

"There's nothing to know, Mr. Stowers, because you have the wrong woman."

"Did you set up an account on a DNA site recently? A few weeks back?"

"Well, yes, but I'm sure a lot of people do that."

"Have you looked at your results?"

She froze in place again, her heart thumping a million miles a minute in her chest. "No."

"Why don't you go take a look at that, and give me a call when you have a little time to digest the information. I'm sure my number is on the…" Before he could finish, she pressed the end button and walked like a zombie to her laptop.

This just wasn't possible. No way. She opened her laptop and navigated to the website, her hand shaking as she typed in her password.

Within moments, she was staring at her family tree, her closest relative match was a sister.

A sister? She had a sister?

She couldn't catch her breath.

"What's your problem?" Evie said from beside her as she took an apple from the fruit bowl in front of her.

"I have a sister."

"Um, no you don't."

Kate pointed at the screen. "Yes, I do. And some attorney just called me and said…"

Evie stared at her. "Said what?"

"That my birthmother died."

"Your birthmother? But I thought your mother died before I was born? Her name was Helen, right?"

"This makes no sense. How is this possible? The site must have messed up. Maybe they switched my results with someone else."

Evie sat down next to her, obviously interested in this new drama that had entered both of their lives. "So, how are you going to figure this out?"

"I don't know…" Kate continued staring at the screen like the words were in another language. A sister?

"Couldn't you track down your father and ask him?"

The thought made her sick to her stomach. The last person she wanted to talk to was her father. He'd left her decades ago, so what were the chances that he'd be honest now?

"I don't have a clue how to find him."

Evie slid the computer closer and opened Facebook. "What's his name?"

CHAPTER 3

Kate couldn't believe she was looking at a picture of her father. Or at least the man she always thought was her father. Evie had found him within minutes using the social media skills that all teenagers seemed to have.

He looked a lot older, his hair thinning and gray, slight bags forming under his eyes. He was still married to the same woman, and their kids looked to be teenagers now. His profile said he lived back in Rhode Island now, just a town away from where she was sitting at the moment.

"See, that is where he works," Evie said, pointing at the screen. You could find out a lot about a person from social media, which was really scary when Kate thought about it.

"I can't contact him. He made it abundantly clear that he didn't want me to contact him."

"You want me to do it?" Evie offered. Kate chuckled, knowing full well that her spunky daughter would do it in a heartbeat.

"No, but thanks," she said, smiling slightly.

"Mom, you have to do this. You might have a sister. And that attorney said your mother left something to you. This could be our big break!"

"Our big break? What do you think she left us?"

"A yacht? A mansion?"

"In Carter's Hollow? I would highly doubt that," Kate said, laughing.

"Well, we'll never know if you don't get some courage and contact the man, will we?"

She blew out a breath. "Okay, fine. How do I get his phone number?"

"He doesn't have one listed."

"So, how am I supposed to contact him then, technical genius?"

Evie rolled her eyes. "Jeez, Mom, I just showed you where he works."

"You can't be serious, Evie. I'm not showing up at his work. That's a recipe for disaster… and a restraining order."

"Mom…"

"Okay, fine. I'll do it," Kate conceded. She didn't want her daughter to think she was weak. She'd deal with this issue head on, if for no other reason than to show her daughter she was strong.

MIA CUT the peach cobbler into squares and carefully put each one on a plate, wrapping it in plastic wrap before placing it into the refrigerator. Her mother's peach cobbler was always a hit with guests, and with a new crop of people coming in tomorrow, she needed to be ready.

No matter how many times she made it, she still had to look at her mother's recipe, written on a card in her fancy cursive handwriting. She had always been stylish and sophisticated, even for Carter's Hollow. The town, named after her mother's great-great grandfather - Samuel Carter - was a tiny dot on the map. The local grocery store only had ten carts because that would've been considered a stampede if they were all used at the same time.

But the town was her home and the only place she knew. It was lovely all year round, with four perfect seasons bringing equal parts cold and warm throughout the year. Apple orchards and dairy farms made up most of the landscape, with the blue tinged mountains an ever-present backdrop to her life.

As she tidied up the kitchen, she tried to distract herself from the knowledge of Carl calling her long lost sister. She was itching to know how it went, but sure that he would call her once he knew more.

She knew virtually nothing about this woman, aside from the fact that they apparently shared a mother. As she thought about it, she found herself conflicted, wanting to fondly remember her Momma and being angry that she missed all those years with her sister.

Why had she given her up? Why hadn't she told Mia in all those years? She knew how Mia longed to have a sibling, but she would just always say that it wasn't meant to be.

"Good afternoon, bestie!"

She looked up to see Raven, her best friend since elementary, walk through the back door. Raven, sassy since birth, had a thick mane of jet black hair and had recently started wearing a nose ring. She had never fit into the country lifestyle of Carter's Hollow, with her huge curly hairdo and bohemian fashion sense.

"Hey," Mia said, as she continued wrapping peach cobbler.

"Ah, Momma's peach cobbler? I'm gonna need a piece of that." She reached across the counter and stole an unwrapped piece before swiping a fork from the drawer.

"So, what's up?"

"Well, I came over to talk to you about that text you sent me last night."

"Oh, you mean the one where I told you I have a long lost sister?" Mia said, pretending not to care.

"That's so cool!"

Mia stopped her work and looked at Raven. "Cool? My mother lied to me my whole life!"

"Come on, now, Mia. You know your mother had to have had a good reason not to tell you."

"What good reason is there to not tell me I have a sister?"

"I don't know. Maybe we'll never know the

answer to that. But, what I do know is that you have a sister. A real, live sister. You've always dreamed of having a sibling, and now you do. Don't screw it up by being angry at your mother."

She knew Raven was right. She almost always was, although Mia would never tell her that.

"I'll keep an open mind," Mia finally said, wiping her hands on a nearby cloth.

"Good. So, what do you know about this mystery woman?"

"I only know her name is Kate, and she should be about thirty-seven years old. Apart from that, I know nothing."

"You don't even know where she lives?"

"Nope."

Raven sat for a moment and then her eyes went wide. "Oh no."

"What?"

"What if she's a... northerner?"

～

KATE PARKED in front of the building and sat in her car staring at the front door of a nondescript building. How would she ever do this? She'd written off her father, who she now only referred to as Paul, many years ago. She never wanted to need anything from him again, yet here she was, trying to prove a point to her daughter.

She opened her car door and stepped out, the heel of her boot digging into the gravel. Paul had always done work on cars, and it looked like he was still in the same business. The building, in a rougher part of town, was pretty shabby, but she knew he probably made good money. He was just too cheap to fix it up, most likely.

As she walked through the front door and into a small waiting area, she looked around at the wood paneled walls. The place smelled of old cigar smoke and exhaust from the many cars in the bays beyond the glass window. She could see a few men, in dark gray overalls, working on cars, but she didn't see her father at first.

"Can I help you?" a voice asked from behind her. She didn't have to turn around to know who that was.

Slowly, she turned, wondering along the way whether he would recognize her all these years later. Would she still look like the elementary schooler he left behind decades ago?

But there was no recollection on his face. He just smiled slightly, as if she was a new customer coming to get an oil change.

"Do you know who I am?" she asked.

"Um, I don't think so…" he said, his eyebrows furrowing.

"Seriously?"

He stared at her for a long moment before his face changed. The smile vanished, and his jaw clenched. "Kate?" He didn't say her name like a loving father, but more like she was the villain in a superhero movie.

"Hello, Dad." She said it more to annoy him than anything. He probably didn't want anyone knowing about that pesky daughter he'd abandoned a couple of decades ago. Even all these years later, she didn't understand his venom toward her. She'd never done anything to wrong him, but it wasn't worth trying to figure it out after so much time had passed.

He pointed to a side office and ushered her in there, shutting the door behind them. She stood with her arms crossed.

"What do you want, Kate? Money?"

"Excuse me?"

"I'm not giving you money," he said with more anger than she'd anticipated.

"I don't want your money, *Paul*," she said, accentuating his name. Now, she was mad.

"Then why did you come here?"

"I'm beginning to wonder that myself," she said, walking toward the door. "No, you know what? I'm not leaving that easily."

"Do you really want me to call the cops, Kate?"

She paused for a long moment, remembering why she was there. She no longer needed this man to be her father. She needed information, the truth.

"No need to call the police. I came here to ask you a question. That's it. Once I walk out that door, you'll never see me again."

He blew out an irritated breath. "Fine. What is it?"

She looked at him carefully, hoping he'd actually tell her the truth for once in her life. "Am I adopted?"

Paul looked more than a little surprised. "Yes, you are."

And there it was. The truth, finally after almost four decades.

"Why keep it a secret from me?"

"I said I'd answer one question, Kate."

"Oh, come on. Don't I at least deserve to know basic information about my own life, Paul?"

He sighed and sat down in his creaky, fake leather chair. "Fine. Sit."

She sat down across from him, taken by how incredibly messy the man's desk was. It looked like a mish mash of old receipts and trash from twenty years ago. He lit up a cigarette, which made her want to run screaming from the building since she was highly allergic.

"Your mother and I were in love for a time. A short time. We found out she couldn't have kids, and to save our marriage, we agreed to adopt."

"So I was just a means to save your marriage?"

"Yeah. And for awhile, it worked. We were so focused on you, we didn't have to worry about the fact that we'd grown to despise each other." She'd forgotten just how brash and unfeeling this man could be.

"And then you left."

"Look, I don't want to hurt your feelings, but I just didn't feel that connection with you. And when I met Carol, I knew I could have a real family with her. My own flesh and blood kids."

Even though he wasn't her real father, it still hurt

to hear him say it. She felt like a knife was going through her stomach.

"Did you ever really love me?" she asked without thinking, immediately wishing she'd kept that question to herself.

"I did."

"How did you just leave your daughter behind?" A tear rolled down her cheek, and she willed it to crawl back up into her eye.

"Because I knew you weren't really my daughter. For my own sanity, I had to just move on."

"I can't believe the words that are coming out of your mouth. You do realize that people adopt all the time? And that they love their kids with every fiber of their being? And that blood doesn't matter?"

"It mattered to me."

Kate stood up. "I hope you've been a better father to your *real* children, then."

Paul said nothing and looked down at his hands. "How'd you find out?"

She turned back, just before walking out the door. "Sorry. I only tell my secrets to my real family members."

~

THE ROOM WAS COLD, even for spring time. Mia assumed that Carl had cranked the air conditioning down a few too many notches, his portly physique holding in too much heat. But, she was petite and thin, and she didn't have much insulation to hold in body heat.

She pulled the cardigan she carried with her out of her tote bag and put it on. This waiting game was killing her. She knew her sister would be there any minute, and she had no idea what to expect. Her hands were sweating, which wouldn't make a very good impression when she shook her hand the first time.

Would they shake hands? Hug? Wave from across the room? How did one act in this situation?

"They just pulled up," Carl said, as he walked into the room. He seemed excited, like it was Christmas Eve and Santa was coming. She was a lot more trepidatious about the whole thing. As much as she wanted a sister, could they really form a bond in their thirties? Or would they end up being like distant cousins?

"Gosh, I'm a nervous wreck," Mia admitted. "My inner thighs are shaking. I didn't even know that could happen." Wishing she hadn't shared anything about her inner thighs with Carl, she looked down and wiped her hands on her capri pants.

Today, she'd chosen to wear a bright pink pair of pants, a simple white t-shirt and her sneakers. No need be too formal. She wasn't the type.

Out of the corner of her eye, she saw a shadow moving down the hallway. She didn't want to appear too eager, so she looked down at the table as Kate entered the room. Finally, when she worked up the nerve, she looked up and saw her very tall sister standing there.

They looked nothing alike. Not even a little bit, from what she could tell without staring. Kate was tall and thin - lanky is what her mother might have called her - and had medium brown hair. Even her skin tone was different as she was more olive complected while Mia was pale.

"Kate?" she said softly as she stood up.

"That's me," Kate said, a slight smile on her face. She had a northern accent, which was one of Mia's fears. Most northerners didn't understand her southern twang and folksy sayings.

"I'm Mia," she said, holding out her hand. Kate took it and just about squeezed her bones into dust.

"Sorry. I've always had a firm grip. I didn't expect you to be so..."

"So what?"

"Miniature," she said, dryly.

Carl cleared his throat, probably trying to break the tension in the room. "If you ladies would both have a seat."

Mia sat back down in her chair, completely let down by their first interaction. This was supposed to be her long lost sister, and yet she already found her to be an abrasive person. Thoughts of getting their nails done together and having late night gossip parties were replaced in her mind by Kate trying to kill her while she slept.

"So, you dragged me here from Rhode Island, Mr.

Stowers. What's the big secret that my abandoning birthmother left for me?"

Mia felt rage well up inside of her. "Excuse me!" she said, standing up again, her jaw clenched. "Our mother was a good, decent, hard working woman. You don't refer to her that way!"

Kate glared at her. "Well, excuse me for thinking about her a little differently. The woman left me behind like yesterday's news."

"Ladies, please. This is a very sore subject. I get it."

"Do you, Carl?" Kate said, sarcastically. "Did your birthmother leave you in a basket by the river?"

"What?" Mia said.

"I think she's just being dramatic for effect, Mia," Carl said, waving his hand.

"Well, who knows how I was left? I don't know my story at all because I only just found out I was even adopted. Excuse me for being a little emotional about this whole thing." Kate sat back against her chair and crossed her arms.

Mia wanted to feel bad for her, to feel empathy. But right now all she felt was anger at someone talking badly about her mother.

Carl, sensing they needed to move on from the tension, opened the wooden box he'd had sitting on his desk since Mia first came in to ask him about her sister. He pulled out the same envelope Mia saw the day she met with him.

"Charlene was my client for a very long time."

"Charlene?" Kate said.

"Oh, that's your mother's name."

"She wasn't my mother," Kate said, dryly.

"Birthmother, then. Anyway, many years ago, she told me about you, Miss Miller. And she gave me something to read to the both of you in the event you ever met."

"If she went to all this trouble, why didn't she just find me herself?"

"She tried a couple of times. Used social media, but had no luck. Couldn't really afford a private investigator at the time."

Kate sighed. "Go on."

"Okay," Carl said, cutting his eyes at Mia. He opened the envelope with a letter opener and put on his reading glasses before clearing his throat again. Mia was going to suggest some allergy medication to him after this whole thing. "Here is what she wrote…"

To my daughters,

I know this whole thing is going to come as a huge shock to both of you, and that's why I want to explain.

When I was sixteen years old, I found myself pregnant. He was my high school sweetheart, and we were over the moon excited. Of course, we weren't prepared to raise a baby, either one of us. We were immature and had stars in our eyes, but that wouldn't have made for a good set of parents for a precious baby.

When I told my parents, they were angry. My boyfriend's parents were the same. We thought about running away, but in the end I knew we couldn't take care a baby. We didn't even have jobs. Somewhere in my young mind, I knew what I had to do.

My boyfriend got sent away to military school, so then I was all alone in making the decision. I never saw him again. I truly loved him, so I knew my baby was made with love. It always seemed like enough, but it wasn't.

When I was seven months along, my mother took me to an adoption agency and basically forced me to sign papers. She said either sign them or be disowned. It was an awful day.

The adoption was private because my mother said it had to be that way. I never knew who adopted my baby, but I named her Gwendolyn. She was beautiful with chubby cheeks and green eyes. She was very long, so I bet she's tall like her father.

For years, I wondered and worried about her. When I turned twenty, I found myself pregnant again with Mia. I was now an adult and got to make my own decision, and I wasn't about to let her go. I spent my life scrimping and saving to take care of her, trying to prove to myself that I could be a good mother. And I think I am.

If you're reading this letter, it's because my daughters are together now. It also means I'm not there to see it, and that breaks my heart. But maybe I orchestrated it from heaven because nothing would make me happier than seeing my baby girls get to be sisters. It was my dream for so many years.

Gwendolyn, or whatever your name is now, I love you. I've always loved you. I'm so sorry I couldn't keep you, but I pray you had great parents and a wonderful childhood.

Mia, I'm so sorry I never told you. I just couldn't bear

to see you long for your sister and not be able to find her. I also feared you'd hate me forever if you knew that I gave her up. I guess all of that makes me a coward.

The reason I'm writing this letter is to apologize, but also to tell you something important.

Sweet Tea B&B was my life for a long time. I adore that place, and I know my spirit will stay there forever. It's a part of me. The only way I know how to truly be with both of my daughters is to split the business right down the middle so that you each own fifty percent of it.

"What?" Mia suddenly yelled out, standing up again.

"Mia, please. I need to finish. Just give me a few more minutes, okay?" Carl said looking over the top of his glasses.

She slowly sat back down.

I know this might upset you, Mia, but I want you and your sister to have a chance to bond, to really get to know each other. And I hope she'll get to know me a little bit through you.

So, here is what I propose. I will give fifty percent ownership to each of you. At the end of six months, either of you can choose to sell the business to the other, but to no one else. But you must live together at the B&B for at least six months.

If both of you want to sell, you can make that decision after six months, although I hope that doesn't happen.

If both of you choose to stay, I hope it's because you love my B&B and each other.

I know this will be hard and challenging, but family is worth it. Please do this for me.

Love,

Mom

"This is insane!" Mia said, standing up again. "I've worked side by side with my mother for years. I helped make it what it is today, and now I have to give up half of *my* business?"

Kate looked at her. "Thanks for the welcome, sis."

Mia sucked in a sharp breath and blew it out. "This has nothing to do with you."

"Um, it seems that it does."

"Surely you can see that this isn't fair," Mia said, her face on fire.

"Well, don't worry because I have absolutely no intention of staying here in Hooterville or running that podunk B&B of yours. This trip was a big waste of time."

"Excuse me? Hooterville?"

"Oh, I'm sorry. It was Hooter's Hollow, right?"

"You know dang well it's Carter's Hollow!" Mia said, Carl running out from around the desk to hold her back.

"Ladies, this is unbecoming!" he said, loudly, as the two women snarled at each other like caged cheetahs.

"What is going on in here?" a teenage girl asked from the doorway. Everyone froze in place.

"Who are you?" Mia asked.

The girl grinned. "I guess I'm you're niece."

CHAPTER 4

*K*ate couldn't believe how angry her pixie of a little sister could get. She looked like a freaking preschool teacher, but she was behaving like a professional wrestler. At least she was until Evie showed up in the doorway. Something about seeing her new niece calmed her down enough that Carl could finally put her on the ground, which was a good thing because he looked like he needed a heart pill with his red, ruddy face.

"Niece?"

"Hi. I'm Evie," she said, walking over and holding out her hand. Kate didn't know what game her daughter was playing, but she knew she was up to something. She always was.

Mia smiled slightly. "I didn't know I had a niece. How old are you, sweetie?"

"Fifteen."

"Well, you're just beautiful. I'm Mia."

"Nice to meet you." Oh yeah, Evie was suddenly on her best behavior.

"Evie, we're leaving," Kate said, grabbing her daughter's arm and pulling her toward the door.

"Leaving? We just got here!"

"And now we're leaving," Kate repeated, trying in vain to pull her daughter out of the conference room.

"Mom, I'm tired. That was a long drive. Can't we just stay tonight, at least?"

"No.

"Please?"

"Fine. Where's the closest hotel?" she asked, looking at Carl.

"Darlin', we don't have hotels around these parts. Just farms, mostly. And, of course, the B&B." She looked at Mia.

"Oh, no thanks. We'll drive to Atlanta and stay there then."

"Mom, come on. I'm so tired."

"You're a kid. You don't get to be tired."

"Please, stay with me tonight," Mia suddenly piped up, her eyes wide like she was surprised at what she'd just said.

"What?"

"Look, I know we got off on the wrong foot, but I'd really like to get to know my niece… and you. One night won't kill you."

Kate wondered if the little elf that was her sister could be homicidal, but she was too tired to care.

She honestly just wanted a place to lay her weary head.

"Fine. One night. And then we'll head back home and forget all of this ever happened."

"Excuse me, ladies, but we need to discuss the business…" Carl said, holding up the letter Charlene had written.

"Later, Carl. This was all a little much to handle at once, okay?" Mia said, giving him a look of warning. Carl quickly nodded his head. Kate got the feeling he wasn't the best attorney and would probably fall to pieces in front of a real judge.

They walked out of the office and onto the sidewalk. Never had Kate felt more out of place in her life. Even the surroundings didn't match her personality. There were mountains and farms and the occasional little mom and pop shop. She was used to yachts and tennis clubs and high end clothing stores. Of course, she didn't have the money for any of those things, but she planned parties for people who did.

"I'm in the VW Bug," Mia said.

"Of course you are," Kate mumbled. What else would this tiny woman drive but one of she smallest cars made. And, it was pink. Seriously? She was like a little fairy.

Mia glared at her. "Can we just try to get along? For your daughter's sake, at least?"

Kate looked over at Evie, who seemed to be enjoying the whole thing. She was going to wring her neck later.

"Of course. We'll follow you."

"Can I ride with Aunt Mia?" Evie asked, a grin on her face. This kid was up to no good, for sure.

"I'd love that!" Mia said, smiling. She put her arm around Evie and pulled her close. "I can't wait to get to know more about you, Evie."

As they walked toward Mia's car, Evie looked back at her mother and smiled. This wasn't going to end well.

~

MIA PULLED into the driveway of the B&B. It was long and winding, giving her more time to talk to her new niece. She'd always dreamed of being the cool aunt, and now was her chance, even if she had to deal with Evie's mother. The woman was an Amazon, her head almost touching the clouds. Okay, maybe that was a little overstated, but why was she so dang tall?

"You live *here*?" Evie asked, as she stared out the window at the tall mixture of oak and pine trees dotting the property.

"I surely do! What's it like where you live?"

"Fancy. Over priced. Lots of women with faces that don't move and lip fillers. Snobby people. And the occasional tree."

"Yikes. I could never live someplace like that."

"Why don't you want us to live here, Aunt Mia?" she asked, out of the blue. Mia felt a pang in her heart.

"What?"

"I heard the argument you had with my Mom. It sounded like you weren't happy about her getting half of this place and us living here."

Mia smiled sadly. "It was just a shock, hon. That's all. Your momma and I will work it out, I'm sure. For now, I'm looking forward to showing you Sweet Tea B&B!" They pulled up in front of the property, and Evie's eyes opened wide.

"Wow. Look at this place! It's huge!"

"Yep, it's pretty big. We have ten rooms we rent, in fact."

"I've never stayed at a bed and breakfast."

"Well, now you can cross that off your list of things to do. Come on!" Mia jumped out of the car and stood in front of the B&B, her arms outstretched over her head. "Welcome!"

Evie giggled. "You have a lot of energy."

"I've always been told that," Mia said, smiling. "Momma used to say I had ants in my pants."

"That's my grandmother, right?"

Mia poked her bottom lip out and put her hands on Evie's arms. "Oh, darlin', I wish you could've met your grandmother. She was an amazing woman. So strong and funny. She even had hair like you," she said, running her fingers through Evie's smooth mane of hair.

"Really?"

"Yes. And those freckles on your nose. I bet you get those from her too."

Evie touched her nose and smiled. "I've always wondered about that. Mom doesn't have them."

As if on cue, Kate finally pulled down the gravel driveway. When she got out of the car, she wrinkled her nose as she looked around and then tapped her feet on the ground, looking at the gravel.

"Have you ever thought about paving this?"

Mia rolled her eyes. "Well, do you have about ten grand laying around to do it?"

Kate shrugged her shoulders. "So, this is the infamous bed and breakfast. Pretty nice."

"Pretty nice? Come on, Mom. This place is amazing!"

Kate looked at her daughter for a long moment and then leaned in to get her tote bag from the car.

"We've got a light load of guests today, so I'll put y'all in one of the nicer rooms. We call it the Savannah. Follow me."

The sun was starting to set, and Mia needed to prepare dinner for her few guests. Tonight was chicken and dumplings with salad and cherry pie for dessert. Of course, sweet tea would be the beverage of choice. Charlene's sweet tea was one of their guests' favorites. Something about the way she made it was special and different. Mia wasn't convinced she had the same gift.

Kate and Evie followed Mia to the front door. She never locked it, so she just opened it and walked inside.

"Wait. You don't lock the doors here?" Kate asked.

Mia laughed. "There's no crime around here. People trust each other."

"Well, that's scary," Kate muttered.

"Mom…" Evie groaned. "Can you try to be positive about all of this?"

"You and I are going to have a talk later," Kate whispered.

"Come on in," Mia said, hanging her purse on a hook behind the check-in desk. "Your room will be number eight. Here's the key. It's upstairs on the left, just past the main bathroom."

"We don't have our own bathroom?"

Mia smiled. "No. Only one room has a private bath. It's our suite, but the Rancourt's are staying in it for their honeymoon. We don't see them a lot, if you get my drift."

"Ugh," Kate said, rolling her eyes. "Come on, Evie. Let's take our things upstairs."

As Evie and Kate disappeared up the stairwell, Mia finally let out the breath she'd been holding for the last half hour. She really liked her niece so far, but that sister of hers had been a big letdown. It was like she was determined to be negative about everything.

Of course, Mia felt embarrassed about her outburst at Carl's office too. She'd just lost it when Kate talked bad about her mother. But what would her mother tell her to do? Kill them with kindness. She'd said it all the time.

And, honestly, how would she feel in Kate's shoes? Maybe angry. Maybe sad. Maybe negative.

She tried, in her mind, to put herself in that position.

This whole situation was going to be dicey, and Mia hoped she hadn't gotten in over her head.

~

KATE OPENED the door to their room and stepped inside, Evie following behind her.

"Wow," she said, her mouth hanging open. "I feel like I just landed in the middle of Gone With The Wind." The room was decorated right out of the Civil War time period, complete with thick, heavy drapes on the window and glass table lamps painted with flowers.

"This is so cool," Evie said, grinning from ear to ear as she put her bag on the bed. She pulled out her phone and took a couple of pictures, including a selfie with the huge four poster bed in the background.

"What is going on with you?"

"What do you mean?" Evie said, innocently.

"Come on, Ev. I know you better than anyone in this world, and I know when you're playing a game. I just don't understand why."

"I just want to get to know my aunt. Why can't it just be that simple?"

Kate rolled her eyes. "Because nothing is ever that simple with you."

"I really like Aunt Mia. Don't you?"

Kate's jaw clenched. "She tried to pummel me at the attorney's office."

Evie giggled. "She's pretty fierce for such a little person. But, what did you expect her to do? You were pretty ugly about Grandma."

"Grandma? Aunt Mia? You don't even know these people! Why are you so interested?"

"Mom, this place is amazing. Did you see how big it is? Your birthmother wants to give you half of it. Do you know how much money this place is probably worth?"

"It's in Coon Dog Hollow, Evie. Not New York City."

"Carter's Hollow. Stop saying things like that. You're going to screw up this opportunity for us."

Kate studied her daughter carefully. "I'm not here to cash in, Evie. This is about the fact that my whole life has been a big lie. You need to understand this isn't fun for me."

Evie's face changed in a way Kate hadn't seen before. She looked empathetic for the first time in a long time. "I know. I'm sorry, Mom. I guess I'm just really excited for a fresh start. I've never had an aunt before, and she seems cool."

Kate laid back against the mattress and stared at the ceiling fan. "Cool isn't all that's required here, kid. There's a lot of water under this bridge."

Evie laid down beside her mother. "I'm just saying can't we give Mia and this place a chance? Enjoy this one night and see where it takes us? Maybe we'll be pleasantly surprised."

Kate chuckled. "I guess stranger things have happened."

~

MIA CALLED up to each of her guests for dinner, something that the regulars were quite accustomed to. Of course, the newlyweds didn't respond or come downstairs, so she didn't expect to see them until breakfast. It was times like these when she wished she had a man to lean on, to stay holed up with in a room for days on end, blocking out the world and all of its problems.

All she had was her cat, and he wasn't all that friendly. In fact, he still hissed when she tried to pick him up after owning him for years. Such was her life.

As Mia stirred the chicken and dumplings, she felt butterflies in her stomach. How was she supposed to have dinner with her long lost sister, wayward niece and a bunch of guests without having an anxiety attack? This whole thing was just too much to bear. How could her mother leave half the B&B to a virtual stranger, even if she did come out of the same womb?

"Something smells good," Evie said as she and her mother walked downstairs. Kate said nothing and just walked into the kitchen.

"This is your grandmother's chicken and dumplings. Famous around these parts," Mia said, smiling at Evie. She already liked having a niece, even if she seemed a bit rough around the edges. She would turn her into a Southern belle if she had the chance.

"Not her grandmother," Kate mumbled under her breath.

"Excuse me?" Mia said.

"Nothing."

She decided to let it go, not wanting another dramatic scene to happen in front of her niece. Taking the high road was something her mother had taught her well. She didn't always do it, but at least she knew about it.

"Ya'll can have a seat at the table," Mia said, pointing at the large, rectangular oak table her mother had bought for the B&B right when it opened. It had always been her favorite piece of furniture in the place, with its occasional marks and scratches left by guests - or their kids - over the years. Charlene had said it gave the table "character", and Mia could see that now.

"Good evening!"

Mia turned to see one of her favorite guests, Dave Callahan, walk into the kitchen. He walked over, kissed the top of her head and laughed in his own boisterous way. Dave had been coming to stay at the B&B for years, always showing up the same date each year - May 15. Mia had always wanted to ask him why he came on that date and no other, but she didn't want to pry. She was more in the habit of letting guests reveal things about themselves in their own time. She was only there to make their visit special, and Dave always left with a smile.

"Well, good evening yourself," Mia said with a smile. She hoped to have the warm, welcoming personality her mother did so that guests would come back year after year. Living in such a rural place, she felt like these people were her extended family.

"I see we have some new friends at the table tonight," he said as he walked over to Evie and Kate. "My name's Dave. And you are?"

"I'm Kate, and this is my daughter, Evie."

"Lovely to meet you," he said, tipping his fedora hat before sitting down. Dave was an older, very Southern man with still a hint of an Irish accent. His parents had emigrated to the United States when he was, as he called it, "a wee laddie", but Dave was still as Southern as they came.

"Nice to meet you too," Kate said.

Mia carried a large bowl of chicken and dumplings to the table, steam rising from them, condensation wetting the glass bulbs on the breakfast room light fixture above. She handed Evie a large spoon. "Dig in!"

As they started filling their bowls with the dumplings, Mia brought a pitcher of sweet tea and some homemade biscuits to the table, along with apple butter.

She watched Kate stare at the food for a moment before pouring herself a glass of tea. "So, are there other guests?" she asked.

"We have the newlywed couple, but they are…

um… keeping to themselves," Mia said, cutting her eyes up at Kate.

"Gotcha."

"Oh, I remember what those days were like. My late wife and I were romantics too. Those first years of marriage were heaven on Earth," he said, a smile on his face.

"What was her name, Dave?" Mia asked.

"Ellen. She was a beauty, I tell ya. Beautiful auburn hair, porcelain skin, full rosy lips and the best laugh I've ever heard. She was something else."

"When did she die?" Evie asked, suddenly.

"Evie! I'm so sorry, sir," Kate said, giving her daughter a look.

"Aw, no, that's alright. It's a valid question, young lady. She died thirty-two years ago."

Everyone stopped talking for a moment, until Evie popped up again.

"Did you ever get married again?"

"No, ma'am, I surely didn't. You see, when you've found the love of your life, there's no need to look for anyone else. Nobody could've measured up to my Ellen."

"So, you've spent all these years alone?"

"I have friends back home, of course. And two nieces who still look in on me every week. My church friends have become like family too."

"But no wife or even a girlfriend? Doesn't that get lonely?" Evie prodded. Mia had never seen a kid her age asking so many personal questions. It was kind of making her uncomfortable, except that she wanted to know the answers from Dave too. Curiosity is a strong feeling.

"Evie…" Kate growled under her breath. Mia could certainly see a dynamic between Kate and her daughter. Evie was always pushing past the limits, and Kate was trying to drag her back. Entertaining to watch, but probably tough on her sister.

"It's really fine. I like an inquisitive kid. Makes me have hope for the future of this world. No wife or girlfriend, but I live a happy life. And I love coming here every May."

"Why May?" Evie asked as she slathered apple butter on her biscuit, but not before smelling the sweet substance.

Dave smiled, a faraway look in his eyes. "Back when we were kids, my Ellen and I actually met at a summer camp here. We were just twelve years old, but I remember it like it was yesterday. Because both of our mothers also worked at the camp, we had to come a couple of weeks early to help set things up. May fifteenth was the first day I set eyes on the love of my life. She was standing by the water, skipping rocks across like a professional. I was so impressed. Of course, this structure we're in wasn't built until years later. We were in a large cabin that used to sit right on this spot, though. So, it just feels like home when I come here and look out at the still waters of the lake. I can be with Ellen when I'm here."

Mia felt horrible that she'd never heard that story. All of the years she'd known Dave, and she had never asked him why he always came on the same date each year. Now it made sense why he spent so much time out by the lake.

"That's a beautiful story, Dave," Mia said, smiling as she reached across the table and squeezed his hand.

"That's really cool," Evie said. "Maybe I'll meet my Prince Charming out here in the Georgia woods."

"Your mother gets first dibs on any handsome mountain men," Kate said, offhandedly. She started to laugh, but stopped herself and popped a piece of biscuit into her mouth. Mia couldn't understand why she was so intent on being miserable.

The rest of dinner was mainly Dave and Mia talking, with Evie occasionally making another teenager-ish comment here and there. Dave eventually decided to go to bed, after filling his stomach with plenty of cherry pie, one of his favorites that her mother had made every time he came.

She wondered if Charlene knew the story of why Dave always stayed on the same date every year. But surely she would've shared that info with Mia. She certainly didn't share the news that she had a sister, so maybe her mother wasn't as open as she'd always thought she was.

There was a part of her soul that ached every time she thought about her mother. They'd been so close, almost like best friends. Why hadn't she confided in her? Why had she kept something so important away from her? It made her sad and mad at the same time. So many years wasted when she could've looked for Kate. But, right now at least, it didn't seem like Kate really wanted to be found.

"Goodnight," Mia said as Dave slowly walked up the stairs. Only seeing him once a year meant she could see him aging in front of her eyes. She worried about the year when he wasn't going to show up. The cycle of life and death seemed so much more real these days.

"Well, we'd better go to bed too," Kate said. "We'll need to get an early start tomorrow." She didn't make eye contact with Mia as she gently guided her daughter toward the stairs.

"Mom, why can't we just stay here awhile?" Evie said.

"Bed, Evie. I'm tired, and I don't want to talk about this right now."

Evie sighed. "Fine. Goodnight, Aunt Mia," she said, smiling slightly as she walked up the stairs. Kate mumbled goodnight and disappeared too.

This wasn't at all what Mia had expected, if one could even have an expectation of what finding a long lost sister was like. The loss she felt over her mother passing away was huge, but now she felt another kind of loss. The possibility of finding and then losing her only known blood relatives was just salt in the still open wound on her heart.

CHAPTER 5

*K*ate stared up at the black sky, the moon shining down brightly on the still water in front of her. She took in a long, deep breath - like the one her yoga teacher had taught her - and blew it slowly out of her mouth.

The last twenty-four hours had been a lot to take in. Meeting her sister, finding out she could be part owner in a B&B out in the north Georgia woods, trying to keep her daughter in check. All of it was weighing on her, which was why she was standing outside at two o'clock in the morning staring into the blackness.

She sat down on a bench affixed to a small dock. This was quite possibly the quietest place she'd ever been, with only the sound of crickets to let her know she was still alive and breathing. In any other situation, she would've been scared to be outside alone at this hour, especially in the middle of the forest. But, for some odd reason, this place didn't feel scary to her at all. At the moment, she felt like the only person on the planet.

As far as she knew, Evie was fast asleep right now, after dozing off watching videos on her phone. How she was managing to get a signal out here was beyond Kate. She had enough trouble getting cell service in the city, much less in a place like this. Maybe some kind of mountain magic was involved.

Of course, there was always the possibility that Evie had snuck out and was halfway to Atlanta by now. Her daughter was a bit hard to figure out these days, something that kept her awake most nights. Tonight, it wasn't Evie that was keeping her up. It was her sister, Mia. Or rather her conflicting feelings about her new sibling.

She'd wanted a sister her whole life, and now that she had one, she couldn't wait to get away. In her mind, this whole thing was a mistake. Traveling all the way to Georgia to meet a very annoying little Southern belle wasn't something she'd planned to do. She liked her routine. There was no way she was uprooting her life to live out in the woods and have strangers staying in her home. Nope. Not happening.

And Mia didn't want that anyway. After the way she'd reacted at the attorney's office, Kate had learned her sister had a fiery temper for someone in such a small body. She didn't need more drama in her life. Evie was enough.

Plus, how on Earth would she run a party planning business in a remote place like this?

Still, she needed money. God willing, Evie would go to college in a few years, and she had no college fund for her. Times had always been tough, and sometimes the ends just didn't meet. Being able to cash out her half of the business in six months would give her what she needed for Evie's schooling one day.

Six months. That was a *long* time. And living in podunk USA, it would surely feel like dog years.

"Best seat in the house."

Startled, she turned to see Mia standing behind her, a glass of sweet tea in her hand. Of course.

Without asking, she walked around the bench and sat on the other end, her plush bathrobe pulled around her.

"Are you actually wearing fuzzy slippers?" Kate asked dryly.

Mia laughed and wiggled one of her feet. "Momma gave them to me a couple of Christmases ago. She had matching ones."

"Of course, she did."

They sat for a few moments in silence. "Look, I want to apologize for how I reacted at Carl's office. I'm not proud of that little outburst, and I know Momma wouldn't be either."

"I don't blame you, honestly. If some strange woman came and tried to take away my inheritance, I'd get irritated too. Which is all the more reason why you'll be happy and back to normal when we leave later today. I have no plans to stay here."

"I won't go back to normal."

61

"And why is that?"

Mia looked over at her, only the moonlight illuminating her tiny face. "Because now I know I have a sister. And a beautiful niece."

Kate stood up and walked to the edge of the dock, her arms crossed. "I know you might have this romanticized notion of two sisters finding each other and living happily ever after, but I'm a realist."

"What does that mean?"

She turned around to face Mia. "It means that anyone could plainly see that we're two very different people. This sister relationship would never work out. We'd end up mud wrestling in the backyard."

Mia giggled. "Up here, we call it Georgia red clay, although it's actually orange. And it'll stain your clothes like nothing else."

"A little off topic, but thanks for the piece of trivia," Kate said, rolling her eyes.

"I'd really like a chance to get to know you both, Kate. And to share more about Momma with you. I mean, don't you want to know about her?"

Kate sucked in a deep breath and blew it out. "I don't know how to say this without offending you. But, no, I really don't care to know about your mother."

Mia stood up, her head cocked to the side. "You don't want to know about Momma at all? Don't you have questions?"

"Do you even have the answers?"

They stood there staring at each other for a long

moment. "Fine. But, even if you don't want to know about Momma, what about me? I'm innocent in all of this, Kate. Just like you are. Don't we deserve to see if we can form a friendship, at least? Doesn't Evie need as much family to love her as possible?"

"I have a life, Mia. A job, responsibilities, an apartment. I can't just walk away from that. I don't have to stay here for us to get to know each other. We can be friends on social media or something."

Mia looked disappointed. She sat back down and stared off into the black water. "I remember when I was about eight years old, and I was getting bullied at school. I don't know if you've noticed, but I'm a little…"

"Short?"

"I prefer petite. Well, anyway, I was sitting on the school bus one day, and this big boned heathen named April plops down next to me. She was the worst of the bullies with her fire engine red hair and ginormous freckles. She was as tall as her father, who was a former linebacker for the Atlanta Falcons back in the day. Anyway, big April sits down so hard, I swear I almost popped up like a wine cork and flew out the window."

Kate couldn't help but laugh. "That's quite an image."

"Momma always dressed me up for school. She said you only get one chance to make a first impression, so every single day she pulled my hair up into these beautiful, long pigtails and then braided them. She'd tie ribbons in my hair to match my dress that day. That particular day, I was wearing a sky blue dress with a lace smock."

"Sounds like something out of the pioneer days."

Mia chuckled. "Momma loved to sew, but she didn't always make me the most fashionable clothing. Anyway, this particular day, big April was in a mood."

"Why?"

"Who knows? Somebody probably stole her Twinkie or something. But, she came on the bus already aggravated like some kind of wild, hungry animal at the zoo."

"You paint quite a word picture," Kate said, sitting down beside her.

"Everybody on that bus, including the driver, seemed to be scared of big April. This particular day, she chose me as her prey. When she sat down, I knew it wasn't going to be good. I tried to ignore her, look out the window, stop moving so maybe she'd think I was already dead. Didn't work."

"What did she do?" Kate couldn't believe she was so interested in this completely random story Mia was telling in the wee hours of the morning in the middle of the woods.

"First, she tried to shake me down for snacks. But, Momma was pinching pennies in those days, hence the homemade clothes, and I didn't have anything left but a half a bag of cut up apples. And they were already brown. And big April was not amused. She snarled at me like a rabid raccoon."

"Do rabid raccoons snarl?"

Mia chuckled. "I would assume. Anyway, I shook in my seat as I looked up into the nose hairs of the scariest giant I've ever known. I felt like a little mouse about to get squashed. She told me that I'd better find something in my lunch bag or else. I said I didn't have anything. I even opened my bag, but that didn't do a thing. She was turning all shades of red."

"So, what happened?"

"Well, I tried to get up and move. I was going to sit with the nerdiest guy in our school, Walter Timmons, but big April would have none of it. She wouldn't let me pass."

"Why didn't you yell for the bus driver?"

Mia's eyes widened. "Haven't you ever heard that snitches get stitches?"

Kate laughed. "That's a new one for me."

"The whole bus ride, big April was on me like white on rice. She wouldn't let up calling me names, making threats. I was so scared. When the bus got to my stop, I stood up. Big April stood up too, and I was so thankful because I thought she was going to let me go. Instead, she stepped out and then followed me off the bus. I was normally the only one who got off there."

"Why didn't the bus driver stop her?"

"When I got older, I found out big April's daddy, the former football player, was buddies with our driver. And even he seemed a little scared of her."

"Wow."

"Anyway, so I start walking as fast as I can toward

home, but I've got these little legs and big April was hot on my tail. I tripped over a tree stump and fell flat on my face, giving her the perfect opportunity to pin me to the ground."

"Oh no."

Mia took in a deep breath and blew it out. "She reached into her backpack, took out a pair of scissors and cut off one of my braids."

Kate put her hand over her mouth. "Oh my gosh, Mia! You must've been devastated."

"I was," she said, her eyes watering a bit. "I loved my long hair. It took me ages to grow it out, and everyone complimented me on it. Now, here I was with one long braid and the other one cut right up to my scalp. Big April skipped away - well, as much as she could skip - swinging that braid around in the air and cackling like a lunatic."

Kate truly felt horrible for her, but it went beyond that. She felt a sort of rage she didn't expect. It had been decades since this had happened, yet she had a sudden urge to find big April and push her off the nearest cliff.

"I'm so sorry that happened to you."

"I laid there on the grass, under this huge oak tree, and cried for what seemed like hours. I didn't even care if she came back because I was broken. I ended up having to cut my hair short like a boy, and I was bullied the rest of the year. Momma went to the school and complained, but all big April got was a couple of days of after school detention. Momma had to leave work every day to pick me up from school because I was so scared to ride the bus."

"Why are you telling me this sad story?" Kate finally asked.

Mia looked over at her. "Do you know what I was thinking the whole time I was laying on that ground, looking up into big April's massive nostrils?"

"What?"

"I sure wish I had a big sister to protect me."

Kate wanted to cry, and she wasn't a crier. She didn't like to show emotion at all. "Mia…"

"Look, I know we got started off on the wrong foot. But, I really want to get to know you both. I think we can build our own kind of family."

"I have a life…"

"Just a week. One week. Can you give me that?"

Kate thought for a moment. A week was basically like taking a vacation. No promises or commitments.

"Okay."

"Okay?" Mia said excitedly, a big grin on her face.

"Okay. One week."

Without warning, Mia scooted over and hugged her. Kate just sat there, still like an ice statue. Yeah, emotions were hard.

"I promise you won't regret it," Mia said.

Oh, how she hoped that was true.

~

Mia rushed around the kitchen, trying to get breakfast ready for her guests. The newlyweds wanted it delivered to their room, of course. She hadn't seen them much since they'd checked in, and it made her a little envious. She wondered if she'd ever have someone in her life like that.

Staying up late talking to Kate had caused her to sleep through her alarm, so this morning would be an easy and quick breakfast of pancakes and cheese grits. Not exactly a winning combination, but it would work.

"Mornin'," Dave said as he walked into the kitchen.

"Good morning, Dave," Mia said, wiping pancake batter off the counter.

"You seem a little flustered this morning," he said, smiling.

"It's been a crazy couple of days."

"Oh yeah. Why's that?"

Mia looked at the stairs to make sure her sister wasn't coming. "That woman, Kate... Well, she's my long lost sister I never knew I had. And Evie is my niece."

"Long lost sister? That must be quite a story."

"It is. Momma gave a baby up for adoption when she was seventeen. I never knew about her until I did one of those online DNA tests."

"Wow. That's something else. You just never know what secrets someone is keeping."

Mia shrugged her shoulders. "I know. I'm a little upset that Momma never told me."

He smiled. "Sugar, we all have our secrets. Things we might be ashamed of or embarrassed about. Your Momma probably didn't want to bring up that kind of pain."

"I suppose so. But, you know, my sister and I seem awfully different. I mean, she was raised up north…"

"Oh, the horror!" Dave said jokingly, putting his hand over his heart.

Mia laughed. "Don't you worry. I have a week to turn her into a southerner, and you know I'll die trying."

Dave chuckled as Kate and Evie appeared on the stairwell. He zipped his lips and turned around.

"Good morning, ladies!"

"Good morning!" Evie said. Kate smiled, but she looked very tired.

"Sorry we're a little late. I overslept a bit."

"Me too."

"Mom says we're staying a week," Evie said, grinning.

"And I'm so excited!" Mia said, clapping her hands. "I can't wait to show you how the B&B works, take you around town, maybe even do some hiking."

"Hiking? Yeah, we're not really hikers," Kate said, sitting down at the breakfast table.

"We have some of the most beautiful hiking trails in the world around here. The views are breathtaking."

"Come on, Mom. Live a little," Evie groaned.

"We'll see," Kate said, pouring herself a cup of coffee from the carafe on the table. She loaded it up with cream and sugar until the mixture was almost white.

"Well, you ladies have a great breakfast," Dave said as he stood up.

"Wait, you're not having breakfast with us?" Mia asked.

"Not today, but I'll be back before dinner. Doing a little fishing in the river."

"Oh. Well, have fun and bring back something we can eat," Mia said with a wink.

She had to admit, she was glad to have her sister and niece to herself for awhile. She wanted to learn more about them, figure out what made them tick.

She put a large platter of blueberry pancakes on the table and then a bowl of cheese grits. "Sorry I don't have biscuits this morning. Time got away from me."

"Don't you just pop them out of one of those rolls. You know, the ones that make you think they're going to explode?" Evie asked.

Mia smiled. "No, sweetie. We do everything from scratch here. All from my Momma's recipes. She was an amazing cook."

"What did she look like?" Evie asked.

"She was beautiful. You remind me of her, especially your cheekbones. Actually..." Mia said, standing up and walking to a small desk in the living room. She pulled out a small photo album and opened it. "Here she is."

Evie took the album and stared at it. "Wow. She does look a lot like me. Look, Mom," she said, turning the album to face Kate. For a moment, Kate looked away like she was uncomfortable. But then she eased up and finally looked at the picture.

"I can definitely see a resemblance," she said softly. It occurred to Mia that this was the first time Kate was seeing her birthmother, and she wasn't going to get to hug her. She could only see a photo, and the thought made Mia well up with tears.

Evie turned the page and laughed. "What is this?"

Mia stood over her, looking at the photos. "Oh, that's your grandmother's Halloween costume a few years ago. She wanted to be a princess, but she ended up looking like a drag queen. We had a good laugh over that one."

"Was she funny?" Evie asked. Mia was so glad she was interested in knowing about her grandmother. She felt like it was her duty to fill in those blanks.

"Oh yes. She had a great sense of humor and loved playing practical jokes on me growing up. We were like best friends."

Kate moved uncomfortably in her seat. "So, what's on tap for today?" she suddenly asked.

Sensing that she was pushing too hard, Mia redirected her attention to Kate. "Well, I'd love to take you into the town square, maybe get lunch later?"

"That sounds fun, doesn't it, Mom?" Evie said.

"Sure. So, tell me more about this place, Mia. What kind of revenue do you do?"

"Um, well, Momma handled all that, really. I'm just getting around to looking at the books."

Kate's eyes were wide. "That's really important if you want to keep the business running."

"I know. It's definitely not my forte, though," Mia admitted.

"Mom, maybe you can help her. You're great with numbers," Evie said. Kate cut a look at her.

"I'd be glad to take a look."

"Great. Maybe tonight once I feed everyone."

"Don't you get tired of cooking?" Evie asked.

Mia chuckled. "Occasionally. But, cooking reminds me of Momma, and that helps. Plus, I don't have a family to cook for."

"So, you've never been married?" Evie asked.

"Evie, honestly, stop asking people personal questions!"

"It's okay. She's my niece," Mia said, smiling. "She can ask me anything. No, I've never been married. I was engaged once, a very long time ago."

"What happened?"

"Well, we just wanted different things, I guess. We were young, just out of high school."

"I can't imagine getting married so young."

"It was a good thing we didn't, I suppose. We weren't ready. So, Kate, what do you do for a living?"

"I'm a party planner."

Mia stared at her. "Really?"

"What's so shocking about that?" Kate asked, laughing.

"Momma was a party planner and caterer for a long time before buying this place."

"Wow, Mom. You must've gotten that from her," Evie said, nudging Kate.

"Maybe. Can you pass the maple syrup, please?"

Sensing Kate was uncomfortable talking about her mother, Mia passed her the syrup and quickly changed the subject.

CHAPTER 6

*A*s Kate walked along the tiny square with Mia and Evie, she wondered how anyone could live here. There was nothing to do. No freeways, no malls, no fancy coffee shops. It was like a hometown from the olden days, and she felt very removed from society. And the quiet was deafening. She'd never really understood that saying until now. She longed for the sound of a car horn.

Still, she was enjoying the time away from her business and responsibilities. Thankfully, or maybe not, she didn't have any parties to plan in the upcoming weeks. She would need to get some stuff on the books soon, or her savings would run out. It was a bit worrisome that June was almost there and she hadn't booked any wedding receptions. Summer was prime wedding season.

"And there's the bistro. Ya'll ready to eat?" Mia asked. They'd spent most of the morning shopping in the little speciality shops in the square. First, there was the homemade soaps and essential oils shop where Kate had started to get a headache from all the smells. Turned out, you *could* have too much lavender.

Then, there was the candy store where Evie watched them make fudge and Mia had bought her a big enough bag to keep her awake for years to come. Finally, they'd gone to the candle store where they'd watched a woman make hand dipped candles that smelled like tobacco. A little weird, but interesting.

"I'm starving," Evie said.

"Seriously? You ate your weight in pralines and fudge an hour ago," Kate said, laughing. "I swear she's more like raising a growing teenage boy than a girl."

"Not funny," Evie groaned. "My brain is still growing, and these boobs aren't going to grow themselves," she said, pushing her small cleavage upward.

"Evie!" Kate said, slapping her arm and looking around. Mia couldn't contain her laughter.

"I thought it was funny," Mia whispered to Evie. "And, unfortunately, the women of our family don't get big bosoms."

"Bosoms?" Evie said.

"Boobs. We get average sized ones, but we get very nice skin that ages well."

Evie rolled her eyes. "Great. I'm sure all the boys are looking for girls with nicely aging skin."

They continued walking and talking, and Kate couldn't help but enjoy it. She liked watching Evie interact with Mia, but a part of her was a bit jealous. At home, her daughter definitely didn't treat her the same way. She was abrasive, irritable and almost like a scalded dog at times.

As they walked into the bistro, Kate looked around. It was a cute enough little place, but definitely not fancy. There was a black and white checkerboard floor, dated floral valances and little metal bistro tables scattered around in no particular pattern.

"They have the best Cuban sandwiches here," Mia said, looking up at the menu printed on the wall above the cash register.

Kate ordered a tuna sandwich with a side salad, Mia got the Cuban with a cup of soup and Evie ordered a loaded baked potato. They all sat down to wait for their food.

"So, what do you think of our little town so far?"

Kate struggled with what to say. "It's... quaint."

Evie rolled her eyes. "Jeez, Mom. That's all you can say? Aunt Mia, I think this place is awesome. It's so cozy and quiet."

Kate looked at her daughter. "Since when does a fifteen year old like quiet?"

She shrugged her shoulders. "I didn't know what I was missing. I could totally see myself living here."

Mia grinned. "Really? Oh, that would be amazing! Maybe Evie could just stay for the summer?"

"No," Kate said, probably a little too firmly.

"Oh. I'm sorry. I shouldn't have pushed," Mia

said, standing up. "I need to add a little more ice to my tea. Excuse me."

"Mom, do you have to be so rude?" Evie growled.

"What is going on with you?"

"I don't know what you mean."

"Evie, you're playing games. I know it. You know it. I just don't understand your angle."

Evie took a big bite of her potato, enough to overly fill her mouth, and smiled at her mother as Mia came back to the table.

They ate silently for a few moments before Kate felt guilty. "Sorry I seemed short with you. It's just that I couldn't be all the way in Rhode Island and leave my daughter in Georgia for a whole summer."

"I get it," Mia said, smiling slightly. "I guess I'm just a little over zealous. I've never really had family around, other than Momma."

"Let's just enjoy our week together and see how things go, okay?" Kate said, trying to buy some time.

Mia nodded. "No pressure. Really. I know this is new for all of us."

"So, how is business going with the B&B?" Kate asked, happy to change the subject.

"Good, I suppose. I mean, we get the same folks year after year, which is great. But, I'd really like to grow the business. Maybe branch out a bit."

Kate took a bite of her salad and was pleasantly surprised. "Branch out how?"

"Well, I'd love to start doing weddings."

"You've never had weddings there?" Kate was surprised about that.

"No. Momma was always scared to do them. They're such a big commitment."

"Much like marriage," Evie said with a laugh.

"True. There's just a lot to do with setting up the area for the ceremony, catering, music, taking care of guests… I'd want things to be perfect for the couple, but me doing all of that alone is impossible."

Kate knew exactly what went into a wedding. She'd planned a few for friends, and she'd certainly handled her fair share of wedding receptions. There were a lot of moving parts, which meant a lot of room for errors too.

"I saw a gazebo on the cove of the lake. Seems like that'd be a perfect spot to have the ceremony. That flat area would be great for chairs, and you have some shade from the trees there too."

Mia smiled. "Sounds like you've got it all figured out."

"Side effect of the job I have. Oh, and that huge back patio would be great for the reception. You could easily put tables there, have the food inside and get a portable dance floor for the garden area next to it."

"That all sounds great in theory, but I don't have the expertise for all of that. I'm a little overwhelmed now that Momma's gone. She could run the place in her sleep. I have to think about everything now."

"Maybe you could hire someone?"

Mia shook her head. "I wish, but I know we don't have the extra money for that."

"Hey, hey, hey!" a woman said from beside them.

She had a mane of thick, dark hair, a very 90s retro outfit and a big smile on her face. Mia stood up and hugged her.

"Ladies, this is my best friend, Raven. This is my new sister, Kate and her daughter, Evie."

"Wow! So nice to meet you guys. Mia was super pumped when she found out about y'all. Welcome to Carter's Hollow, by the way."

She pulled up a chair, turned it backwards and straddled it.

"Raven and I have been besties since we were little kids."

"Nice to meet you," Kate said, shaking her hand.

"Those are cool shoes," Evie said, pointing at the neon pink and white retro sneakers Raven was wearing.

"Thanks! I got them at the thrift store on the edge of town. I've found some amazing stuff there."

"I'd love to go sometime!"

"How about now? Y'all game?"

"I'm not much of a thriftier, but you guys go ahead," Kate said. She had never liked thrift stores. The thought of wearing someone else's castoffs just wasn't appealing to her.

"No, I wouldn't dream of leaving you here," Mia said, shaking her head.

"Listen, I don't mind. And I know you want some time with Evie. I can take your car back and hang by the lake until you get home."

"I can drive us in my Jeep," Raven said, holding up her keys and smiling.

"Are you sure?" Mia asked Kate.

"Absolutely. I'll grab myself a cup of coffee and head back to the B&B soon. Maybe I'll map out more of the wedding ideas so you'll have them when I leave."

Mia smiled. "That would be great."

"Wedding ideas? Who's getting hitched?" Raven asked.

"I'll explain in the car," Mia said, standing up and handing Kate the keys to her car. "If you need anything, just text me."

As they left, Kate took the last few bites of her food and looked around. Maybe there was a way to build a relationship with her sister. They were very different, but she was starting to feel more comfortable. Of course, the other part of her wondered what might be coming next.

~

KATE FINISHED her meal and walked down the sidewalk. The town was cute, she had to admit. The air was also very crisp up in the mountains even though it was May.

She sat down on a bench under a big oak tree and looked down at her phone. A text message popped up. It was a customer back in Rhode Island, wanting to know if she could plan a retirement party for the father of a wealthy socialite. The party would be held in a mansion in Newport.

As she looked at the text and then looked around

Carter's Hollow, she almost had to laugh. The two areas of the country were so vastly different.

Daddy must have the best lobsters we can find. Perhaps you have connections in Maine? Also, the table-cloths are a big issue for me. I don't like cheap materials. Nanette said you did well with her party last year, but I was there and those tablecloths were atrocious. Can you speak about that?

Ugh. Sometimes she hated the types of people she had to deal with in her business. They were typically snooty, uppity and beyond annoying. But they had money, and she needed it.

Still, when they went home to their mansions, nannies and often loveless marriages, she went to a tiny apartment where the stove only occasionally worked and the upstairs neighbor seemed to wear tap shoes day and night.

Sometimes, it wore on her. She wanted more, for herself and her daughter. She wanted stability, financial freedom and peace. She wanted to look in her bank account at the end of the month and not have a panic attack trying to figure out how to make ends meet. She wanted to not pressure her daughter to find her first job just so she wouldn't have to give her so much spending money anymore. She wanted to be able to say yes when Evie wanted to see a movie or take hip hop dance lessons.

She said no a lot.

"You okay, miss?" a man asked from beside her. He was standing over her, a cup of coffee in his hand. She glanced up, not long enough to even see his face, and then looked back down at her phone.

"Yes. Thanks."

Without warning, he sat down on the other end of the bench and sighed. "Sure is pretty weather out here today, huh?"

She didn't make eye contact. "I guess so."

He cleared his throat. "You new in town?"

Finally, she looked at him. He was handsome, no doubt about it. But he wasn't handsome in a Newport, Rhode Island kind of way. He was mountain man handsome, with hands that had seen real work and tan skin that didn't come from a spray or a booth.

He had brown hair with tinges of gold, and it was so thick that she was jealous. It hung just above his shoulders, and she tried hard not to look lower at his biceps bulging under the cotton t-shirt he was wearing.

"Um, yes. Just visiting, actually."

"Ah. Well, welcome to Carter's Hollow."

"Thanks," she said, looking back down at her phone. She started to type a response about the tablecloths.

"How long have you been here?"

"Are you writing a book?" she asked, looking at him again. Cute or not, he was becoming a little intrusive.

"Sorry. I guess my granny was right when she said curiosity killed the cat. It's just you look a little like a fish outta water with your fancy purse and staring at your cell phone."

"I'm sure other people around here have cell phones," she said, dryly.

"True enough. We just don't look at them so often."

"Thanks for the input," she said, looking back down.

"My name's Cooper," he said, reaching his hand in front of her. She stared at it for a moment and couldn't help but notice he wasn't wearing a wedding ring. Of course, it didn't matter, but somehow it seemed important in the moment.

"I didn't ask."

He chuckled. "You from up north?"

Again, she turned and glared at him. "What difference does that make?"

He smiled. "Just noticed your accent is all."

"Oh. Yes, I'm from Rhode Island."

"Never been there before. Is it nice?"

"I like to think so."

"Are you going to tell me your name?"

She sighed. "Kate. And I don't want to be rude, but I'm kind of busy here."

"Got it," he said, sitting back and yawning. "I'm just taking a break from work. I like to come do a little people watching."

She looked back and forth. It was a weekday, and there were a grand total of three other people on the square. One was washing store windows, one was an old lady with a walker and the other was a man hanging up a flyer on the front of a store.

"There are no people."

Cooper laughed. "I didn't say it was successful people watching. So, what are you doing here in our very boring little town anyway?"

"I'm visiting my sister, if you must know."

"Family's important."

"Yep." She looked back down at her phone, scrolling to make sure she hadn't missed any other messages when her cell service wasn't the best.

"What do you do?"

"Huh?"

"For a job? What do you do?"

"You ask a lot of questions, Cooper."

"I like how you say my name," he said with a wink. She wanted to smack him right across one of his adorable dimples.

"I have a boyfriend," she said, lying.

"I didn't ask you about a boyfriend."

"Okay, but I thought you should know."

"Why?"

"Because you're clearly hitting on me."

He chuckled. "Men up north must not be so nice."

"Excuse me?"

"This is just how we shoot the breeze down here, Katie."

"Kate."

"Right. Anyway, I wasn't asking you on a date. I mean, what makes you think I don't have a girlfriend?"

"Well, I don't know…"

"I mean, I'm clearly handsome," he said, smiling as he leaned back and flexed his muscles.

"Wow," she groaned.

"And, as you can tell, I'm a great conversationalist."

"Absolutely," she said, rolling her eyes as she stood up.

"Hey, where ya going?"

"Away," she said before walking down the sidewalk.

As she made her way to Mia's car around the corner, she could feel him looking at her, and it made her want to smile more than she'd ever care to admit.

CHAPTER 7

"So, do you like school?" Mia asked Evie as they looked through racks. So far, Evie had found a pair of jeans, some cool vintage sneakers and a pair of earrings that hung almost to her shoulders. Mia had offered to buy everything, not that she had a ton of extra cash lying around. She just wanted to be the cool, fun aunt, even if it was only for a week. She had to make memories so Evie would want to come back one day.

"Not really. It's kind of a bore," she said, picking up a red crop top and holding it up to her chest.

"Um, no," Mia said. "Your mother would kill me."

Evie rolled her eyes and hung it back up. "I love this band tee."

Mia quickly looked at the price tag and nodded. "A dollar I can do. So, what do you want to do after high school?"

"I don't know. Maybe travel."

"Travel? Where?"

"I want to, like, backpack around Europe. I saw a YouTube video about that, and it seems fun."

"Right," Mia said, pretending to look at clothes. "But, if you don't get your education, how will you pay for that?"

"It's cheap. You just camp as you hike. No biggie."

"Got it. And your mother is okay with that idea?"

Evie laughed. "My mother isn't okay with pretty much anything about me."

"I'm sure that's not true."

"It's totally true. She rides me about every little thing. It's so annoying."

"Y'all, look at this skirt? Can you even imagine me wearing this? It's amazeballs!" Raven said like a giddy schoolgirl. Mia would swear she got stuck in her teenage years sometimes because she sure didn't act like a thirty-four year old woman.

"Nobody says amazeballs anymore," Evie said.

"Cool people do," Raven retorted before going back to the dressing room.

"I was thinking about what you said about your mother riding you. You know, I'm sure she means well. She wants to protect you. That's what mothers do," Mia said.

"She just wants me to be something I'm not."

"And what is that?"

"Perfect."

"Does it make my butt look too big? I mean, I know that's in right now, but I don't want my cheeks hanging out," Raven asked, turning around and trying to see her own hind quarters.

"It looks fine," Mia said, giving her friend a look of warning. Raven backed into the fitting room and pulled the curtain closed. "Have you talked to your mom about your feelings?"

Evie chuckled. "You don't know Mom very well yet, but she isn't the easiest person to talk to. She's stubborn as a mule."

"That might be genetics," Mia said, smiling. "Look, mothers love their daughters. Just tell your Mom what's going on in that teenage head of yours so she can help."

Evie turned and looked at Mia. "I appreciate the advice, Aunt Mia. I really do. But can we just have fun shopping? You're being kind of a downer."

"Right. I wouldn't want to be a downer. Come on, let's go look at the belts."

~

KATE STOOD in the living room, the first time she'd been alone in the B&B since getting there. From the lack of cars outside, it seemed everyone was gone for the moment, so she sat down on the sofa and stared at the mantle. Pictures of her birthmother were everywhere, like some kind of photo memorial to the woman that left her behind all those years ago.

It wasn't like she didn't have a decent upbringing. Her mother had been good to her, but she'd always felt a little out of place. She didn't look like either of her parents, and now she knew why. She was taller, by several inches, than her mother, and the kids at school hadn't always been kind about that.

She stood and walked over to the desk, picking up a silver framed picture of her birthmother. It looked recent as her hair had flecks of gray. She had to admit she was a beautiful woman with her auburn tinted hair and porcelain skin. Her resemblance to Evie was uncanny, and it made something in the pit of her stomach churn. How could she miss a woman she'd never met and only found out existed a few days ago?

As she put the picture down, she turned to see another framed photo at the end of the mantle. It was her mother and Mia, standing together and smiling. The Christmas tree was decorated behind them, snow in the window just beyond. She wondered what Christmases would've been like as a family. It made her ache a bit to think of what she'd missed with her mother and sister. She didn't want to feel that way. She wanted to compartmentalize her feelings like she always did, but it was proving difficult.

The B&B felt like home, in a way, but also like she'd been dropped onto another planet. She walked to the kitchen and looked around. It was hard to imagine that her mother had been standing there a few months ago, possibly using the pink retro mixer on the counter. She touched it, running her fingers along the cool metal, trying to connect with her mother's spirit. What was she really like? What would she be thinking right now if she could see

Kate - who she'd named Gwendolyn - standing in her kitchen?

Her eyes inexplicably welled with tears as she thought about this mother she would never meet. Why was this suddenly bothering her so much? She didn't even know the woman. She never would. All of this was useless emotional energy that she could not afford to lose. She needed to stay strong for her daughter, be the kind of mother she needed.

Kate walked over to a rocking chair in the corner of the living room. A handmade throw blanket was laid across it. Mia had mentioned in passing that her mother had made the blanket while she was sick, a new hobby she had taken up to pass the time and try not to think about her cancer.

Against her better judgment, she picked up the blanket and sat down in the chair, pulling the soft, woven fabric up to her face. She took in the smell of it, wondering if it was the scent of her mother. A mixture of lavender and something else she couldn't identify wafted up into her nose and caused her eyes to well again. Why was she doing this to herself?

"You alright, sweetie?"

She turned to see Dave standing in the foyer. How hadn't she heard him come in?

Quickly wiping away a stray tear, she put the blanket down in her lap and smiled. "Oh, you scared me, Dave."

He walked over and sat down across from her on the sofa. "Sorry, dear. I just got back from fishing."

"How'd it go?"

"Let's just say we'll be eating chicken tonight."

Kate laughed. "They weren't biting today, huh?"

"Not on the end of my pole, they weren't. Listen, when I walked in, you seemed upset. Is everything okay?"

She paused for a moment, considering her answer. "You knew my mother, right?"

He smiled broadly. "Oh yes. Charlene was salt of the Earth."

"Really?"

"Yes. I loved her like a daughter. Watching her go through that damn cancer was one of the hardest things I've ever had to see. She fought for two years. I remember when I came back last May. She was already so frail, but danged if she didn't still make the peach cobbler and sit with me to chat every evening."

"I guess I'm having a hard time connecting with her."

"I know I'm a stranger to you, but can I offer some advice?"

"Sure."

"Be open to this experience. Charlene is here. She's in every part of this beautiful place. She's in that peace lily plant over there. I remember when someone gave that to her a few years back, and she kept it alive, even when it looked like it was about to kick the bucket."

Kate laughed. "I don't have a green thumb myself."

"Me neither," Dave said with a chuckle. "But

Charlene exuded life in everything she did. See that painting over there? The one of the covered bridge?"

"Oh yeah. That's beautiful. I love the colors."

"Charlene painted that."

"She did? Was she an artist?"

"Self taught, but like with her knitting. She was something special, that one."

"I never knew I was adopted."

"Yeah, Mia told me. That's rough stuff."

"If I had known even a year ago, I might have met her before she…"

Kate couldn't believe she was opening up to this man. He was a stranger to her, really, but somehow that seemed to make it easier. Why was this bothering her so much? She didn't even know the woman. How could she miss her so deeply and yet still feel angry toward her?

"Regrets are hard. But, here's the silver lining as I see it. You have right now. You're here, in the place she loved, with your sister. The smell of her perfume still floats around this place. Everything she touched is still here. Make that connection while you can. Why do you think I come here every year? It connects me to my Ellen, even though she's up there in heaven. I know she's also here."

"Thanks, Dave. I really appreciate it."

He smiled. "Well, I'd better get upstairs and take a nap before dinner later. Old men like me love their naps."

She nodded as she watched him walk upstairs and disappear. Could she really make a connection with her mother by just being at the B&B? And did she even want to go down that road?

~

MIA STOOD there with the phone up to her ear, her eyes wide as her sister looked at her with concern on her face.

"What date are you looking for?" she asked the woman on the other end of the line. "End of July? Okay…" She looked at her schedule book and penciled something in. "Can I give you a call back later today after I do a little planning? Great. Thanks."

She pressed the end button and stood there, frozen in place.

"What's wrong?" Kate asked.

"I just got offered a huge wedding for the end of July."

"And that's a bad thing?"

"Well, when I have literally no experience planning a wedding of this magnitude, yeah. But, the bigger deal is *who* it is."

"Who is it?" Evie asked, a grin on her face.

"Someone famous."

"What? Seriously? Who?" Evie pushed.

"Lana Blaze."

Kate and Evie's mouths dropped open.

"Oh my gosh! That's amazing!" Evie said. Even Kate, at her age, knew how huge Lana Blaze was. She'd had one of the biggest pop albums of the year and was predicted to win several Grammys.

"How on Earth did Lana Blaze even find out about this place? I mean, no offense but it's not exactly well known."

"That was her personal assistant. She said Lana stayed here as a little girl with her family. Of course, I have no clue who they were since that's her stage name. Anyway, she remembered Momma and was sad to learn she'd passed away. She really wants the food we made for her back then, and she loved the location since she wants to keep her wedding out of the press. What better way to do that than come way out to north Georgia and into the woods?"

"This is literally the coolest thing that's ever happened! I mean, it's freaking Lana Blaze! I can't wait to tell my friends..." Evie said, pulling out her phone.

"No! Evie, you can't do that. At least, not until after Lana posts about it after the wedding. She's trying to keep this a secret, remember? You have to promise me," Mia said, putting her hand over Evie's phone.

Evie sighed. "Okay. Sorry. I promise, I won't post a thing. But, I must get a picture with her!"

"Ev, you know we won't be here in July," Kate said.

"I can't do this. There's no way," Mia groaned before falling onto the sofa face first. Her nose and lips pressed into the fabric.

"Why?" Kate asked.

"Because not only have I never done a wedding, there will be a good hundred people here, and it has to be done secretly. I can't handle all of these moving parts. If I get this wrong, I could destroy the business Momma built. It's just not worth the risk."

"Mom…" Evie prodded.

"I'll help you," Kate said. Mia pushed herself up to a seated position and looked at her brand new sister.

"What?"

"I'll help you make this happen."

"But how?"

"We can start planning now, and maybe I can come back in July. If not, we can video chat…"

"Or we can just stay for the summer…" Evie said, smiling.

"Ev, we can't do that. I have work back home. And you probably have summer school."

"Come on, Mom. You don't have work like this. It's Lana Blaze! And I'll do classes online. They already said I could."

Mia stood up and walked to the desk, picking up a notepad where she had written some things while she was on the phone. "Look," she said, handing it to Kate.

"What's this?"

"That's the amount they're offering if we do this wedding, plus a twenty percent bonus if we can pull this off without the press finding out."

Kate's eyes widened. "Seriously? They're willing to pay *this*? I'm obviously in the wrong business. Who has this kind of money?"

Evie grabbed the notepad and her mouth dropped open. "Lana Blaze has this kind of money. Mom, we can't go home now. How cool will it be if I can say I helped plan Lana Blaze's wedding? It's a once in a lifetime opportunity!"

"I don't think I can do this without you, my long lost sister," Mia said. "And we can split the profits from this fifty-fifty."

Kate sat down and sucked in a long breath. "We'd need to have some extra structures built out back to accommodate that many people. And possibly a covered pavilion in case we get any helicopters or drones flying over trying to get a shot."

Mia smiled. "Does this mean y'all will stay until the wedding's over?"

Kate looked over at her daughter and then back at Mia. She sighed. "I'll have to give up my apartment…"

"Our apartment sucks anyway, Mom," Evie said.

She laughed. "That's pretty accurate. Okay! I'm in! Let's do this crazy thing."

Mia screamed and hugged her sister. "This is going to be so fun and also terrifying!"

"Definitely terrifying," Kate said under her breath.

∼

KATE WALKED into the tiny gym, a water bottle in one hand and her phone in the other. When she'd asked Mia whether there was a place to work out in town, she hadn't expected this little hole in the wall to be it. It was one large room with machines covering every square inch, and it was also a virtual ghost town. Didn't people exercise in Carter's Hollow?

"Hey there! Welcome. How can I help you?" the perky young woman said from behind the desk.

"I'm just visiting, but I was looking for a place to workout."

"Fantastic! We have a free two-week special going on, and then it's ten dollars a month after that."

"Ten dollars? How do you stay in business?" Kate asked, her mouth hanging open.

"Um, what?" the woman asked, her head cocked to the side. Kate imagined she had a couple of squirrels playing the fiddle inside her brain, so she decided not to press it further.

"Nevermind. Where do I sign up?"

The woman handed her a clipboard and pointed to a chair. Kate sat down and filled out the short form before handing it back in. Finally, she was free to go exercise, and she needed to burn off some excess energy anyway.

Dealing with canceling her lease with her landlord and hiring a moving company to take her things to storage had taken up a couple of days. Thankfully, one of her friends back in Rhode Island had coordinated much of it for her. Of course, she'd have to find a new place to live all over again once she got back home.

She stepped onto the treadmill and started it off

on a low speed. She wasn't exactly a fitness enthu-
siast even back home, but she felt the need to burn
off some excess tension. Besides, she'd been eating a
little too much peach cobbler this week at the B&B.
If nothing else, she had to give it to her mother for
being an amazing recipe writer.

Popping in her wireless earbuds, she turned on
her favorite playlist, turned up the treadmill speed
and tried to escape the world for awhile. After
fifteen minutes, she'd had enough and slowed down
her pace to a more reasonable level. Something
about pushing herself hard helped shake off her
anxiety about all of the things going on in her life.

She worried about Evie, of course. But she also
thought about how awful it was that her daughter
had no relationship with her father and how much
that would affect her in the future. She thought
about how Brandon was missing out on knowing a
wonderful girl too.

There were so many times that she felt lonely,
and maybe that was why she was open to this crazy
experience at the B&B. She missed having someone
around other than her daughter. There was little
support back home, and she longed for that.

Although she'd never admit it to anyone, she
watched those gushy chick flicks that came on
around Christmas time and wished she had a man
like that. Someone who could fix things around the
house, cook her dinner on a lazy Sunday afternoon
and walk the imaginary dog with her in the
evenings. Someone who would rub her feet, listen to

her complain about her day and cheer her on to new adventures.

Did a man like that even exist?

Lost in thought, she pressed the button to stop the treadmill, but instead of stopping it she somehow hit a super speed button or something because it took off at a pace she wasn't expecting. The next thing she knew, she was flying straight off the back of the machine. As if the world was in slow motion, she just knew she was going to smack right into the wall a few feet behind her and leave the outline of her butt for all to see. Instead, she landed on something soft, her feet dangling in mid air, two strong arms around around her waist.

As she struggled to catch her breath, the stranger put her down and she turned around to thank him.

"Cooper?"

He smiled. "Well, hello again."

Oh, this wasn't good.

CHAPTER 8

"*Y*ou can put me down now," Kate said, craning her head back to look at Cooper.

That lazy smile he had on his face, the one with the deep dimples that she wanted to stick her finger in, was really irritating. How could he be so handsome and infuriating at the same time?

He slowly lowered her to the floor, keeping one hand on her waist until she stepped back far enough to release it.

There he stood, wearing a gray tank top, shorts and a pair of sneakers. He had just the right amount of sweat beading on his forehead, obviously from doing some kind of exercise that she hadn't noticed during her furious walk on the treadmill.

"What? No thank you for catching you in mid air?" he said with a laugh.

"Thank you." She turned and started to walk towards the elliptical machine, trying to slip her earbuds into her ears before he had a chance to say anything else.

"Do you need me to show you how to work the treadmill? I mean I wouldn't want you putting a hole in that wall. That would be pretty expensive to repair."

She glared at him. "The stupid machine malfunctioned. I know how to work it."

"That's really weird because I use that machine almost every day."

"Good for you. If you'll excuse me, I'd like to listen to my music now."

That did nothing to dissuade him from following her right over to the elliptical machine. He leaned on the handles, his elbows keeping them from moving. He was like some sort of handsome bully that she didn't know whether to slug or ask out to dinner.

"Why do I get the feeling that you don't like me?"

"Because you're perceptive?" she said, sarcastically.

"Listen, I'm really a pretty nice guy. I open doors for people, I pay my taxes, I visit my grandma and I catch women when they're flying across rooms. What more could you ask for?"

Kate leaned forward, getting within a few inches of his face. "Does this routine usually work on the women around here? Because it's not working on me." *Lies, all lies.*

Cooper stood back up and smiled. "I guess I need to up my game, then."

Kate rolled her eyes and started moving, hoping

that he'd get the hint to just walk away. No such luck.

"And, for your information, I just moved back here a couple of weeks ago after being gone for almost ten years."

"You came back to this place? Why?"

He shrugged his shoulders. "Contrary to what you may think, this town grows on you after awhile."

"I would highly doubt it," she said.

"Well, I'll leave ya to it, Katie," he said, turning to walk back to the weight area.

"Kate," she grumbled as she put her ear buds back in. And she might have watched his very toned rear end as he walked away.

～

EVIE STOOD on her tip toes and reached high into the closet. Turning to make sure no one was watching her, she pulled down the box she'd spied a few days before. This house was a treasure trove of interesting things, and she'd never been able to say no to digging for secrets.

Mia had gone out back to look at the patio and grounds so she could start coming up with ideas for construction. Her mother had gone into town, so this gave her the perfect opportunity to look around the house. She was curious about her roots, wanting to know more about her grandmother. But, her mother had seemed against all of it, preferring to know very little about where she came from.

She took the box from the hallway closet and went into her room, setting it on the bed. It was dusty and old, obviously having been in the closet for a very long time. She opened it and found a pile of papers, notebooks and other keepsakes that someone had packed up a long time ago.

First, there was a yearbook from Carter's Hollow High School. Given the date, she realized it must've been her grandmother's. She scanned each page for her name, hoping to see a glimpse of what she looked like when she was her age.

Sure enough, she found Charlene on page sixty-three. Evie ran her finger across the page, mesmerized by how much she really did look like her. Different decades called for different hairstyles, but otherwise they could be twins.

"Evie, did you want something to eat..." Mia said from the doorway. She stopped short and looked at the box. "Where did you get that?"

Evie squinted her eyes. "I'm so sorry, Aunt Mia. I shouldn't have been snooping around. I found it in the top of the storage closet, way in the back."

Mia slowly walked over and sat down on the bed. "It's okay. I haven't seen that box since I was a kid. Momma used to keep it away from me saying she had her personal things in there." She ran her fingers along the edge of the tattered box, Charlene's name written in big black marker across the side.

"Oh. Do you want to put it back up?"

Mia paused for a moment. "No. I think Momma would be okay with us looking through it now."

Evie smiled. "Have you seen this yearbook? Look at how much we look alike!" She passed it to Mia.

"Wow," she whispered. "Both such beautiful women."

Evie dug back into the box, pulling out a yellow notepad with words written in red felt pen. "What's this?"

Mia took the notepad and read some of the words. "These are Momma's poems. She went through a phase where she wrote poems to help her deal with things. Sometimes, she'd give them to me when I was going through something hard."

"What is that one called?"

"It's called "The Me I'll Never Be'," Mia said, her eyebrows furrowing.

"What does that mean?"

Mia read the first part.

The me I'll never be
Is the one taken from me
When you were pulled away
And all I wanted to say
Was please, my baby, just stay.

"Wow, that's powerful," Evie said, softly. "Do you think that's about Mom?"

Mia swallowed hard. "I do."

"What's about me?" Kate asked from the doorway.

Evie looked at her aunt for guidance. "I was snooping around and found this box of Grandma's stuff."

Kate's face didn't change. "Oh. Well, I'm going to take a shower. I just got back from the gym."

She walked toward the closet. "Mom, you need to see this." Evie held out the yellow pad.

"I'm sweaty and tired. I really need to get my shower," Kate said, not looking at her daughter.

Evie stood up and walked to the closet. She held out the pad once again. "Your mother wrote this about you. I think you'll want to read it."

Kate sighed and took the notepad, walking over to the rocking chair in the corner of the room and sitting down. She sat there, staring down at the words, but saying nothing.

"That's really nice," she finally said, handing the pad back to her daughter. She picked up her clothes that she had set in a pile on the dresser and walked out of the room toward the bathroom.

"I don't know what her problem is."

Mia smiled sadly. "We can't begin to understand what she's going through. I mean, here she is at thirty-seven years old finding out her parents aren't who she thought they were. And then she finds her birth mother only to learn that she's passed away. She's got a lot of conflicting emotions, so we just have to give her some grace."

"I guess so. I just think she's going to regret not seeing all of this stuff."

"Look at this," Mia said, holding up what appeared to be a journal.

"What is it?"

"It looks like my Momma kept some journals, from all the way back when she was about your age. This one is from high school."

Mia stared down at the pages, turning each one slowly, her eyes occasionally welling up with tears. Evie wanted to grab it straight out of her hands and read every detail, but she refrained. This had to be hard on her aunt to relive all these memories and find out her mother's innermost thoughts.

"Does she talk about my mom in there?"

"She does. She talks about how scared she is being pregnant. How she doesn't want to tell her mom and dad. How much she loves her baby's father."

"Can I read it?"

Hesitantly, Mia handed her the journal. She wiped away a few stray tears as she watched Evie read it.

I felt the baby kick for the first time today. It's so weird. I never imagined it would feel like this. Keeping this pregnancy a secret is getting harder. My sweatshirts, even the big ones, are starting to get tight. I think my mom suspects something.

"She must've been terrified."

Mia nodded. "I can't imagine. She wasn't even much older than you when she got pregnant. She had your mother at seventeen, but she was only sixteen when she got pregnant. Can you imagine how terrifying that must've been?"

Evie wanted to cry. Putting herself in her grandmother's position made her think about all of it so differently. What would she do if she were in a similar situation? How would she ever give her baby away to strangers? She had a hard time even donating her old clothes to the local thrift store.

"We have to get Mom to read this. It's the closest thing she'll have to hearing her mother's words about her."

"In her own time, Evie. Don't push."

They continued going through the box, finding several other journals from different times in Charlene's life. From the time that she gave her baby away to the days after that. Then they were happy journals from when she met Bobby. But there was a whole huge chunk of time from when she got pregnant with Mia that was missing. Literally, it was like entire journals were gone. Mia felt let down judging by the look on her face.

"We must be missing something. Are you sure there aren't any other journals in there?"

Evie shook her head. "No. Maybe there's another box?"

"Or maybe she just didn't feel the need to journal about me," Mia said, sadly.

"I don't know. It seems like she liked to journal about everything. I think we must be missing one or two."

"Maybe. Well, I was going to make some lunch. Do you want anything?"

"Sure. I could eat a sandwich. I'll be down shortly," Evie said.

Mia walked out of the room, leaving Evie to stare

at the pile of journals and poems. How could she miss the grandmother she never knew?

∼

IT WAS time to say goodbye to Dave, and Mia always hated this part. She'd grown to love the guests that stayed with her each year, and she worried about the day when some of them didn't show up again. Life moved so quickly, and sometimes it wasn't fair at all.

"Have a safe trip," Mia called as Dave pulled away.

"I'm going to miss him," Evie said. She'd really taken to the place way more than Mia ever expected. Kate had told her privately about some of Evie's issues back home, but Mia hadn't seen any signs of that so far. Maybe the B&B was healing her troubled soul.

"So, I have some ideas I wanted to show you for the wedding," Kate said, holding a notepad. "Want to go out back and take a look?"

"Sure," Mia said.

"I'm going to go take a walk," Evie said.

The two women looked at her. "A walk? Since when do you walk?" Kate asked.

"Since there's not a lot to do around here?"

Mia chuckled. "She's got you there."

"Fine. But take your phone and be back in no more than an hour."

"Got it," she said, walking up the gravel drive and out of sight.

"That kid's going to be the death of me," Kate said as they walked around the side of the B&B.

"Oh, she's a doll."

"I love her. I do. But this kid, I don't know at all. She's actually being pleasant. Back home, she was like having a wild animal in the house."

"Over dramatic much?" Mia said, laughing.

"Maybe a little," Kate said, cutting her eyes at her sister.

"Okay, so show me what you've got."

Kate pulled out a notepad that she'd sketched her ideas on. There were drawings and notes all over the place. Mia giggled.

"What?"

"Nothing. You just remind me of Momma."

"Why?"

"She wrote notes just like that. They were all over the place. In fact, she loved to use the backs of the envelopes from bills we got in the mail. She was constantly asking where the phone bill was, but not because she needed to pay it. She had a recipe or something written on it."

Kate smiled slightly. "I do the same thing."

"Genetics are a strong thing, I guess."

"I guess so."

"You know, I'm happy to answer any questions about Momma or anything else when you're ready. I mean, if you're ever ready for that."

"I know. And thank you. This is all new to me, Mia. You had her your whole life, and I'm just not sure I want to open that can of worms. I hope you can respect that."

"I do respect it. So, show me what you're thinking."

Kate pointed to different parts of her drawing as they walked the property. Mia was impressed with her organizational skills and knowledge of what they needed to pull this huge wedding off. She knew for sure there would be no way to do this without her.

"Right here is where I think we should put the dance floor. I think we should hire a local contractor to build it for us. Do you know anyone?"

"No, not really. I'll ask around, though."

"Okay. With the gazebo, I think we should also get someone to extend it so we can have smaller weddings completely inside of it, with the backdrop being the lake."

"More weddings?" Mia asked with a laugh.

"Hey, if we can pull off Lana Blaze's secret wedding, you can certainly host smaller ones, right?"

"We'll see."

"Come on. I want to show you what I'm thinking for the patio space…" Kate said, as Mia followed behind her like a lost puppy dog.

∽

NIGHT TIME WAS Mia's favorite. All of her guests, the few that were there at the moment, were in their bedrooms. The newlyweds had left a couple of days before, and Dave was gone until next year. Now, she had a little down time to reflect on this new experience with her sister and niece.

But mostly she was thinking about her Momma tonight. She wanted to hug her, talk to her, ask her what to do with her life. She'd given the best advice in the world, and now Mia needed her more than ever. How would she ever be able to run the B&B and make it successful if she felt like such an imposter inside?

She was just a tiny country girl at heart, not some kind of business person. As she stared at the spreadsheet in front of her on the laptop, she wanted to cry, eat a pint of ice cream and curl up in a fetal position. Spreadsheets made her more anxious than the bears that roamed the woods around her property.

Needing her mother, she closed the spreadsheet and opened her video folder. One of her guests, a very tech savvy woman, had been kind enough to put all of her videos onto digital. She cherished that file more than just about anything because at least she could see and hear her mother. Often, she'd sit in her armchair, her mothers perfumed blanket in her hand, and watch those video clips while she sobbed. Not an effective therapy, most likely, but she'd felt the need to do it several times.

Sometimes, she yelled at God, asking why He took her away so soon. She was only fifty-four years old. It wasn't fair. One day, if she was lucky enough to get married and have kids of her own, her mother wouldn't be there. Every time she thought about it, she wanted to sob again. Life just wasn't fair.

She opened the first video, one of her favorites. At the time, she was around ten years old. The video showed she and her mother trying to do cartwheels out in the front yard. Bobby was recording them and laughing in the background. Mia giggled as she watched it, remembering how goofy and spontaneous her mother could be.

Not that she didn't worry or freak out from time to time. She was one of those people who smiled and kept it together for everyone else, but Mia would sometimes hear her crying alone when things got tough.

The next video was when Mia was sixteen and learning to drive. She smiled as she listened to her mother's voice as they drove down the road. She was giving Mia tips on her driving skills, but encouraging her at the same time. She just had that way about her, where she could guide someone without making them feel stupid.

Would she ever be as strong a woman as her mother?

"Hey," Kate said from behind her. Mia had been so wrapped up in the videos that she hadn't seen her sister standing there. She slammed the laptop closed and dried her eyes.

"Oh, sorry. I didn't see you there."

Kate smiled and sat down beside her. "Can I see?"

"You want to?"

She paused for a moment. "Yeah. I'd like to know more about my birthmother."

CHAPTER 9

Kate sat beside her sister and looked at the videos on her laptop screen. She had actually come downstairs for a glass of water, and now she was sitting there watching videos of the woman she said she didn't want to know more about. For some reason, she'd felt a pull when she'd seen Mia watching them.

"This one is from when I was about eleven years old. Momma decided to have this big birthday party for me, but we had only been in that school system for a few months. Only one person showed up, and that was because she didn't have any friends either," Mia said, laughing.

"What about Raven?"

"We met right after this, actually. She kept me safe around school. Nobody messed with Raven then, and nobody messes with her now."

Kate chuckled. "Yeah, I can totally see that."

Mia moved to another video. "This is a Christmas video. You see that wreath on the door? Momma made that. She would sell them at the holidays, although she gave more of them away than she sold. I never could make them like she did."

"Is that a go-cart?"

Mia smiled. "Yeah. Bobby, her husband, bought that for me when I was fifteen. We used to ride it all over the trails out there. But then I crashed it right into the lake, and Momma made Bobby get rid of it. She said since I was her only child…" Mia stopped short. "Oh, gosh, Kate. I'm so sorry. I wasn't thinking."

Kate sighed. "It's not your fault, Mia. It's not really anyone's fault, I guess."

"I wish you'd gotten to meet her," Mia said, her eyes welling with tears.

"Me too."

They watched a couple more videos, laughing and chatting. Kate was starting to get more comfortable around her sister. Even the little town was starting to grow on her. She could see potential in the B&B too.

"Can I ask you something?" Kate asked.

"Sure."

"What do you know about your biological father?"

Mia sighed. "Honestly, not much. Momma never wanted to talk about him. When I asked as a kid, she would just tell me my father wasn't in the picture and that she was going to work so hard to be everything I needed. I felt bad asking, so I finally stopped."

"I wonder about my birthfather. Is he alive? Would he want to know me? It's all just so complicated."

"Do you think you want to look for him?"

Kate leaned back in her chair and shrugged. "Maybe one day. But right now I need to process all of this first, if that makes sense."

"I know you lost your adoptive mom, but what about your adoptive father?"

Kate groaned. "We were close when I was little, but my parents divorced when I was in fourth grade. My father left, started a whole new family and dropped me like a hot potato."

"I'm so sorry."

"No big loss to me now, but it sure hurt when I was a kid."

Mia walked into the kitchen and put on a pot of coffee. Even though it was after ten, she needed a little pick me up to get her back into that spreadsheet at some point before she could even think about going to bed.

"What about Evie's father?"

"We were married for a long time. Divorced when Evie was ten. He did the same thing my adoptive father did and started a new family. I think it's why Evie has had some of the trouble she's had. She kind of has a 'get them before they get me' mentality."

"Apparently, we don't have great luck with fathers," Mia said, leaning against the counter. "Maybe that's why marriage scares the crap out of me."

"Oh, you too? I doubt I'll ever do it again. I'll become one of those old maids with forty cats and a lot of muu muu dresses," Kate said, laughing.

"We can do that together!"

"I assume my birthfather is very tall."

"Maybe so because Momma wasn't much taller than me. You got that height from somewhere."

Kate smiled. "This is nice."

"What?"

"I don't know. It kind of feels natural, you know? Like real sisters."

"I didn't want to say anything, but it is nice. I've always dreamed of having a sister, and now you're here. Can I hug you?"

And for once in her life, Kate suddenly felt like she was accepted, so she stretched out her arms and welcomed it. "Bring it in."

～

EVIE STOOD on the edge of the ravine, looking down at the creek running below it. She didn't have places to retreat like this back in Rhode Island. Sure, there was the ocean, but there was no place for her to go out and explore like she did here.

She missed her friends back home, the few of

them that she had. But she sure didn't miss school. Her reputation there had become tainted, and now that she couldn't go there anymore anyway, it just served as a reminder of all the ways she had failed her mother.

Being here, in this place, felt like a new beginning. Although she wished that she had gotten to meet her grandmother while she was alive, she felt surrounded by a gentle spirit that she assumed was her grandmother.

Now, as she stood there looking down the rocky ravine peppered with vegetation, she wondered how she could get down there. Ever since she had been taking her daily walks, she had wanted to get to the creek. But she just couldn't figure out how to do it.

Every day, she came back to the spot and stood there trying to find the best route down to the water. Sometimes, she thought about how cool it would be to have a zip line to take her straight across to the other side. But none of that was going to get her to the bottom.

She tried to figure out which rocks she could step on without slipping and falling, but none of it looked particularly safe. Someday, she would map out a plan of how to get down to the creek. She had most of the summer to do it.

It had been nice to get to know her aunt, and she felt like her relationship with her mother was even getting better. Although, her mother still didn't trust her. Who could blame her? She had done quite a lot of things for a fifteen-year-old.

Ever since she had read some of her grandmother's journals, she had thought about how difficult it must've been to be pregnant as a teenager. She couldn't imagine that. But it gave her a whole new respect for this grandmother she had never met.

She sat down on the ground, her legs dangling over the ravine. She liked to pick up little rocks that she found nearby and toss them straight down into the creek below, waiting to see if she could see a ripple from her perch above.

Until she had come here, she never thought of herself as an outdoorsy person, but she loved being outside now. Most of the time, she forgot to even get on her phone until the evenings when things got a little more boring around the bed and breakfast.

There were always new guests coming and going, some that Mia was close to and others who were new to the place. But it was interesting sitting at dinner each night listening to their stories and learning more about where they were from.

It'd been hard for it to just be she and her mother all these years. She'd longed for family, although she had never said it out loud. Sometimes, she wondered what she was missing.

If she really thought about it, she missed her father. Or the man she wished he was. When the other kids at school had their dads show up for games and recitals, she sometimes hid in the bathroom to cry. Why didn't her father care about her?

They'd been so close when she was little, but as soon as he decided to leave her mother, he'd left her too. She wasn't even a thought in his head, apparently. He'd found a new wife and made a whole new family like she didn't even exist.

The pain was almost too much to take sometimes, so she acted out to distract herself. That's what the therapist had said, anyway. All she knew is that there were dark parts of her brain where she didn't like to go, and thoughts of her father were always there.

Her last therapist had said that she took all kinds of chances doing things that could hurt her because she didn't feel worthy of good things. Maybe that was true. She definitely didn't feel good about herself, although she put on a good front so nobody knew it.

Being in Carter's Hollow had been a great escape for her. She only wished she never had to go back to Rhode Island and the memories there. Of course, the bad part was that memories tended to follow you no matter where you went.

～

KATE FINISHED her workout and walked out of the gym. She hadn't seen Cooper the last few times she'd gone, and it had kind of disappointed her, if she was honest. No way she'd ever admit that to him, though.

She walked outside and took in a long, deep breath of the mountain air. It was beautiful today, the sky a blue color she couldn't adequately describe in words, not a cloud to be seem. The blue tinged mountains that surrounded her were starting to provide a sense of peace, and the air was still crisp even for early June.

Vendors were setting up on the square for a spring festival, artisans of every type dotting the area, sharing their wares. Not ready to go back to the B&B, she sat down on her favorite bench and watched them.

"Fancy meeting you here," Cooper said from behind her.

"Ugh."

He walked around and sat down beside her, a big smile on his face. "Well, that's no way to greet a friend."

"If I see a friend, I'll be sure to greet them," she said, dryly.

"Have you missed me?"

"Have you been gone?"

"Aw, come on, Katie. You know I haven't been to the gym in days."

"Why do you insist on calling me Katie when I've told you over and over that my name is Kate?"

He shrugged his shoulders. "I dunno. I guess because Kate seems so formal, and I'm trying to loosen you up."

She glared at him. "Why are you trying to loosen me up?"

"Because you seem tense."

"I'm actually not tense, thank you very much. You just make me want to scream, that's all."

He laughed. "You're not the first person to tell me that."

"Do you have siblings?"

"Yeah. Two older brothers. Why?"

She nodded her head. "I can see that."

"What?"

"I bet your brothers picked on you. Threw you in the lake, wrestled with you, that sort of thing?"

"That's what brothers do," he said.

"You're overcompensating."

"What's that supposed to mean?"

"It means you think the more manly and macho you act, the bigger you appear to others. But, in fact, it makes you seem kind of like a horse's ass sometimes."

He let out a loud laugh, causing some of the vendors to turn and look. "I love that you tell it how you see it, Katie. It's awesome."

She groaned and started to stand up.

"Wait. Please."

She sat back down. "What?"

"I actually am sorry. You're right. I've been kind of a jackass since we met. Sometimes I can't help myself. My mama always said I had a sharp sense of humor."

"Well, I wouldn't give up your day job to be a comedian or anything."

"That's probably a good idea. Besides, my day job pays pretty well."

"What is it that you do exactly?" she asked, unsure

of why she cared. If he wasn't so handsome, she would've already run the other direction.

"I'm a contractor. I build anything and everything."

A lightbulb went off in her head. "A contractor, you say? Interesting. I might have some work for you, if you can behave yourself."

"I can always behave myself when it involves work. What do you have?"

"I need some structures built. I have an event venue where we are going to host weddings, so I'm going to need a portable dance floor, an extension on the gazebo and some other things. Do you think you're qualified?"

He smiled. "I can build anything you need. Would you like to see some of my work?"

"Yes. Do you have a binder or something?"

Cooper laughed. "No, I'm not that fancy. But I can drive you around town and show you some of the things that I've built."

"Drive me around town? So you expect me to get into the car with a virtual stranger and drive through the mountains?"

"We're not strangers, Katie! I caught you when you flew off the treadmill. That makes us close friends."

She had to laugh at that. "I'm never getting back on the treadmill again. It's evil."

"What do you say? I have some time right now. I can show you three or four things that I've built around here, and then you'll know whether you want to have me come out and give you an estimate or not."

Kate thought about it for a long moment. They needed to get to work on these structures in order to be ready when Lana's people came out to review the site. If they didn't have everything built in time, the wedding would be moved somewhere else, and they would both lose out on a whole lot of money.

"Okay. But I'll have you know that I have mace in my purse and I've taken a self-defense class."

He looked at her carefully. "I know you're joking about thinking I might be an ax murderer or something, but let me tell you something. I'm a southern gentleman. I would never lay a finger on a woman, unless of course she asked me to," he said with a wink.

As they stood up and started walking towards his truck, Kate got shivers she hadn't ever felt before. She might be going down a path she shouldn't, but for some reason she couldn't help herself.

∽

KATE COULDN'T BELIEVE she was riding around town with Cooper. As they chatted in his truck, the wall between them started to crumble. He seemed like a pretty nice guy, if she was being honest. She learned that he'd grown up in Carter's Hollow, but had left a few years ago for a a job in Florida. He'd only recently came back home to be nearby as his parents aged.

It wasn't like she hadn't met men like him before who were trying to be funny but coming off as cocky and a bit rude. In reality, he was just a good old southern guy who probably thought he was flirting.

He pulled down a dirt road, and she thought about pulling the mace out of her purse just in case. Instead, she decided to just go with it and trust that he wasn't going to harm her in any way. When they finally stopped, he got out of the truck and came around to open her door. None of the guys she'd dated, including the one she married, had ever been big on opening doors. She liked it.

"We're in the middle of the woods. I don't even see anything you could've built," she said, still hanging onto the handle of the truck door.

"I know. It's down closer to the river. There's no way to drive down there. Don't worry, I'll help you watch for snakes."

"Snakes? I wasn't even thinking about that!" she said, really wanting to crawl back into the truck and lock the door.

"I've lived in this area my whole life. I promise I won't let anything happen to you," he said. Something about his eyes, his big, brown, beautiful eyes, made her trust him. This was how a lot of horror movies started.

"Okay," she said, her voice a bit shaky. He led her down a path toward the river. She could hear it before she could see it. They had had a lot of rain recently, and it was raging.

As they finally got over to the edge, she saw a huge overlook deck. It was built out of lumber, but parts of it were also built out of tree limbs. It looked like it was meant to be there, nestled in the middle of the woods.

"You built that?"

"I did. The people who own this property wanted a place where they could sit overlooking the river, have family dinners and so forth. Their house is way up there on the hill. You can barely see it."

She looked up and saw a log cabin built into the side of the mountain. "It's beautiful, almost like a piece of artwork. Can we walk down there?"

"Of course. Let me help you," he said, taking her hand and helping her walk down the steep path toward the river. Although she was wearing her workout sneakers, they certainly weren't the best for hiking down a mountain.

They made their way down the hill and onto the platform. She could tell that he did good work. It was sturdy and well designed. It didn't stick out like a sore thumb in the middle of the wilderness. Instead, he complemented it in a way that she couldn't really describe.

"This must've been really hard to build down here. How in the world did you even get all of this lumber down the hill?"

He flexed his muscles and smiled. "You don't think these muscles got built in that rinky-dink gym, do you?"

She laughed. "Well, I have to say I have a new

respect for you. This is amazing. Do you work by yourself?"

He nodded. "Yes. I've never been able to find good help that was reliable and up to my standards. So, it might take me a little longer but I always do everything myself."

"Impressive. I could see myself having dinner here, overlooking the river. It must be beautiful at sunset."

"Tell me when."

"What?"

"You tell me when you would be willing to have dinner with me at sunset sitting right here, and I'll make it happen."

She smiled. "Why don't we go look at the next site?"

They walked back up the hill and got into the truck, Kate's stomach full of butterflies. Had he just asked her on a date? And was she really considering it? This was crazy. First of all, he was totally not her type. Second of all, she disliked him immensely about half an hour ago. And third, she would likely be leaving after the wedding in July, so getting anything started with a local guy wasn't going to be a good idea.

And yet all she could think about was sitting on that platform overlooking the river, clinking a glass of wine with this hunky southern man.

"So, where we going next?"

"It's just down the road a ways. I know you mentioned a gazebo, so I'd like to show you one that

I built." She tried to refrain from looking over at him, but it was hard. The smell of his cologne had recently caught her attention, and she had a sudden urge to nuzzle her nose into his neck while he drove.

What was happening to her?

CHAPTER 10

*M*ia was enjoying herself more than she had since before her mother got sick. When Kate had agreed to spend some time cooking with her and Evie in the kitchen, she thought she was hearing things.

Over the last couple of weeks, they had really forged a bond that she didn't expect when they first met. There was a part of her that half expected to wake up one day and her sister and niece be gone. She didn't think they would be able to have such a great relationship, but it was growing day by day. For the first time since her mother had passed away, she felt like she had family again, like there were people who had her back. People who shared her blood. People who would be her forever family.

As they stood in the kitchen, Mia pointed out everything they needed for the peach cobbler. That had been the one request Kate had. She definitely wanted to learn how to make that peach cobbler, which gave Mia hope that she might have some southern roots in there after all.

"Are you sure we're supposed to use this much sugar?" Kate said, laughing as she held up the bowl.

"You don't question the recipe. That is the first rule of cooking Momma's peach cobbler."

Evie laughed. "I think you could stick a spoon in there and it would stand up by itself," she said.

"Good. Then we know we're on the right track!"

The three of them laughed, occasionally threw a little flour at each other and chatted about life. It was one of the rare days that there were no guests at the B&B. Although Mia loved having people there, if for no other reason than more income, she relished those moments where she got to be alone in the big house. And now, she really enjoyed the moments when it was just the three of them.

Sometimes, she closed her eyes while she sat in her bed at night and tried to imagine what it would've been like to grow up with her sister. Would they have gotten along? Would they have fought over boys, make-up and the blow dryer? What would Christmas have been like? Easter egg hunts? Skipping school with friends just to swing from the rope over the local lake?

A part of her was sad that those years could never be recaptured, but they had right now. And they had a good fifty or sixty more years they could spend together, so she was thankful for that.

"So we're going to use fresh peaches?"

Mia stared at her like she was speaking another

language. "You realize Georgia is the peach state, right?"

Kate laughed. "Fine. It just seems like canned peaches would be faster."

"That's sacrilege! Momma is probably turning over in her grave right now."

"Aunt Mia, what were you like as a kid?"

Mia smiled. "Awkward, quiet, often bullied."

"That's hard to believe now. You're so outgoing."

"I learned to toughen up over the years, I guess. Being so short, I had to develop a thicker skin."

"I have the opposite problem. I was so tall that everybody was scared of me. I was almost this height by the time I was in the sixth grade. I towered over every boy, and I never had a boyfriend until high school."

"Really? I always wanted to be tall, leggy, like a model."

Kate chuckled. "Being tall doesn't necessarily mean you can be a model. Everybody wanted me to play on the basketball team, but I'm just about as coordinated as a drunk rhinoceros, so that didn't work out too well."

Mia enjoyed these conversations. They were about everything and nothing. Having that time together as a family, getting to know each other, was priceless. She truly believed her mother was smiling down from heaven as she watched them.

After making peach cobbler, they decided to work on dumplings. Chicken and dumplings were one of the best, most requested recipes at the B&B.

Mia felt like Kate should know how to make them, just in case she changed her mind and decided to stay on permanently.

She hadn't broached the subject with her lately, not wanting to push too hard. She was thankful enough that she was staying until the end of July to help her with the wedding.

They only had a couple of weeks to get the buildings done, and they still hadn't had a contractor come out. It was starting to worry Mia. In such a small town, it was hard to find somebody reliable who could do the kind of work they needed. The structures needed to look nice, not like something Billy Bob from the gas station had thrown together with two by fours.

"So, we really have to get all these buildings for the wedding underway. Any ideas on how to find someone who can do such intricate work? Maybe we need to expand our search to Atlanta." Mia asked.

"Well, actually, I have somebody coming out tomorrow to give us a quote. He's very talented. I met him at the gym, and I was able to actually go out and see some of his work."

Mia stopped and stared at her. "Are you telling me you met a guy?"

"I'm telling you I met a *contractor*," she said, avoiding eye contact.

"I think you're getting a little red in the face," Mia said, grinning from ear to ear.

"It's hot in here."

"Mom, your hands are shaking. Are you interested in this guy?" Evie prodded.

"I am interested in him coming over and giving us an estimate tomorrow," she said, still not looking up from the dough.

"I think we're embarrassing her," Mia said. "But you can't blame me. I haven't been around for any of your dating escapades. At least tell me whether you're interested in this guy?"

"Okay, fine. He's cute. What's the big deal?"

"No big deal. But I can't wait to meet him. Is he going to be my brother-in-law?"

Kate picked up a handful of flour and blew it straight into Mia's face. Of course, Evie thought that was hysterical, which started a much larger food fight than any of them had anticipated.

They would spend the next couple of hours cleaning up the kitchen and trying to wipe away the explosion of flour that had consumed almost every surface.

∼

KATE SAT IN THE ARMCHAIR, her mother's blanket pulled around her. Even though they had never met, she was starting to get accustomed to the smell of her.

The journal from the time period that she was pregnant with Kate sat in her lap, closed. Kate took a sip of wine and finally picked it up.

Everybody had gone to bed, only she sat up in the darkness, a small table lamp beside her.

She hadn't been able to sleep for some reason. Cooking her mother's recipes with her sister had brought up a lot of feelings she didn't expect to have.

In a way, she was going through some kind of grief that she hadn't expected. When she thought about it logically, it made no sense. She had never met the woman, yet she felt a void.

She had been raised with a mother, even though she had no idea they weren't biologically related. She had had the mother and daughter bond with some-one, or so she thought. But this was different. This felt like a part of her was missing, yet was so close within reach that she could almost touch her.

Finally, she opened and read the first couple of pages of the journal. They were from the time that her mother had found out she was pregnant. She could feel the fear in her words. What must that have been like? To know that her parents were not going to approve, what kind of turmoil must she have felt every single day?

Today, I found out I'm pregnant. I know we should've been more careful, but we are so in love. I haven't told him yet, and I don't know how he's going to feel. What do boys say about things like this? Will he leave me? Will he be forced to?

As she continued to read, tears started streaming down her face. She put herself in her mother's posi-tion as much as she could. To be sixteen years old and terrified, and all alone on top of it.

I told him today. He was so happy! We both are. We have to convince our parents to let us get married and raise our baby. No other choice is even possible. Even though my baby is still a tiny little bean inside of me, I am going to be a mother. I have to protect him or her with everything I have.

She continued reading, right up until the point of where her mother had told her parents. It was agonizing to read the words that she had written after that.

I think they hate me. They're so disappointed. They called his parents, which was really embarrassing. What must they think of me now? I'm a failure. I'm a disappointment to everyone that knows me. I don't know what's going to happen. My parents said they won't agree for us to get married. I overheard them talking about giving my baby away. I just won't do it. I can't. If I have to run far away, then I will.

In that moment, Kate wondered if her mother ever tried to run away. Didn't she have any family that could take her in? Had she tried to start over on her own?

They caught me. I didn't get very far. My mother was crying when they found me down at the bus station. I didn't even have enough to get on a bus, so I don't know why I went there. I was just so desperate. Today we're going to the adoption agency, and I just want to curl up and die. I can't live without my child. I just can't.

Kate wiped her eyes and took another sip of her wine, setting the journal back in her lap. She was glad to be awake by herself because this was something she really needed to do alone. Emotions were hard for her normally, and right now she felt like she was on the verge of a breakdown.

She took a deep breath and picked up the journal again.

There was nothing I could do. They wore me down. They forced my hand. I'll never forgive them for what they're making me do. They'll never understand what it's like to give away your child. And now the love of my life is gone too. His parents sent him away, saying I'm a bad influence. That we can never be together. I don't even know where he is. The only good thing about today is feeling my baby kick, but I'm heartbroken knowing that I will never even get to hold him or her.

Kate wasn't sure she could continue reading. She didn't know how she was going to be able to get through the rest of this journal. A part of her was so angry at the grandparents she would never know.

They took my baby away. I have never felt so empty in my whole life. I never even got to hold her, but they did let me name her Gwendolyn. I don't know if her new parents will keep that name, but I hope they do. I don't know what to do from here. How do I start over knowing that some stranger is raising my baby girl? How do I breathe? How do I put one foot in front of the other? There doesn't seem to be a life in front of me. My parents said they would disown me if I kept my baby, but now I really want to disown them. How will I ever not be angry at them? I have so many questions and I have no answers. Only God can help me now.

Kate closed the journal because it ended there.

She hugged it tightly to her chest, understanding more than ever how her mother had probably grieved for her for so many years. Gone was the anger and resentment she had felt when she first found out. That had been replaced with love and empathy for this woman who had given her life and agonized after being forced to give her to someone else.

She turned off the lamp and sat in the darkness until she finally dozed off, thoughts of her birth mother in her mind and heart.

~

MIA STIRRED batter and poured the perfectly round pancakes into the pan. Kate had told her that the contractor was coming this morning to give an estimate, so she wanted to make sure everybody got fed before that happened.

She was starting to get nervous. The wedding was coming up in just a little over a month, and Lana Blaze's personal assistant was coming out in another week just to make sure things were on schedule and looked good.

Even though the wedding was a big secret, they would want beautiful pictures, so it was important that the contractor had the highest quality craftsmanship. Plus, these structures they were building could be used in future weddings and hopefully provide a great extra income for the B&B.

A lot was riding on this.

"Good morning," Kate said as she came down the stairs.

"Good morning. Did you want bacon with your pancakes?" Mia asked. Having her sister around had become the norm. She was so glad that they had found an ease with each other.

"Sure. I like mine crispy," Kate said as she poured herself a cup of coffee. "Need any help?"

"Nope. I have it covered. We're supposed to get some new guests this afternoon. I think they are checking in around four o'clock."

"Do you need me to get a room ready?" Evie asked from the living room. Mia had shown Evie how to help set up the rooms for new guests as far as making sure the linens were clean and on the bed and that they had fresh towels and washcloths.

"That would be great," Mia said. "Put them in room four. It's got a beautiful view of the lake."

"Do we know who these people are?" Kate asked as Evie went up the stairs.

"From what I understand it's a husband and wife on their anniversary."

"Must be nice," Kate said, rolling her eyes.

"Well, maybe Mr. Contractor will take you on a wonderful honeymoon one day," Mia said, laughing.

"Stop it! I mean, he's hot. There's no denying it. He's muscular, tan and he has the most beautiful eyes that look like milk chocolate. Gosh, I sure love chocolate."

Mia started laughing. "Well hopefully Mr.

Chocolate Eyes will be here on time. Contractors rarely are."

"Oh, I think he'll be here on time. He's a little smitten with me, so I'm sure he wants to make a good impression."

"Well, look who's a little full of herself this morning," Mia said with a smile.

"No, but I have to admit it does feel good to have somebody pursuing me. It's been a long time. And he's a really nice guy, a little cocky but has a great sense of humor. We started off on the wrong foot when we met, but his work and craftsmanship is unparalleled to anything I've ever seen. We would be lucky to get him to do this work for us."

"Well, let's not tell him that," Mia said, putting two pancakes on a plate and sliding them over to her sister. "If there's one thing Momma taught me, it's to never name the number first. Have him give us a number and then we can counter."

"And what if his number is reasonable?"

Mia paused for a moment. "Well, I don't know, but I've never seen it happen."

Kate laughed. She ate her food as quickly as possible. "I better run upstairs and touch up my make up. Wouldn't want to scare the contractor," she said, grinning from ear to ear.

As she ran upstairs, Mia couldn't help but laugh to herself. She hadn't known her sister for very long, of course, but she certainly hadn't seen this side of her. It made her happy to see that Kate had found someone she was interested in. Maybe they would start dating and she'd have yet another reason to stay. The closer they became, the more she couldn't imagine her sister going all the way to the northern end of the country. Sure, they could visit, but it would never be the same as having her live right there at the B&B.

She wiped her hands on her apron and then took it off and hung it on the peg where her mother had always hung hers. She never wore an apron when Momma was alive, but it made her feel closer to her when she put it on to prepare food. Just another little thing to remind her of how much she missed her.

She saw a big red truck pull up in front of the B&B and realized the contractor was actually early. That was a first. "Kate! He's here!" she yelled up the stairs. But she didn't hear anything, so she assumed she might be in the restroom. "I'll get it!" she called back up, sure that Kate probably couldn't hear her anyway.

She walked over to the door and opened it, a big smile on her face. And then she froze.

"Cooper? What the heck are you doing here?"

~

MIA HAD NEVER BEEN SO stunned in her life. It had been years since she'd seen him, and she had hoped it would be many more.

"I asked you a question. Why are you here?"

He looked down at his feet and then back up at her. "I'm... Is Kate here?"

"Kate? How do you know Kate... Oh my gosh. Are you the contractor?"

"Yes. I'm sorry, Mia. I had no idea you were still here. She didn't mention you..."

"She's my sister."

His mouth dropped open. "Your sister? But you don't have a sister."

"Well, I do now. My mother gave up a baby as a teenager that we never knew anything about until we found each other on one of those DNA websites. Not that any of this is your business."

"I didn't put two and two together. I know your mom passed away. I'm sorry about that. She was a wonderful lady."

"Cooper, you need to go."

"When Kate said she was working with her sister, I just assumed you had sold the place and someone else had bought it. If I had known you were still here..."

She put her hands on her hips and cocked her head to the side. "You would've what? We both know that you would've still come out here because that's just who you are. Always have to have your nose in everybody's business. Always have to be Mr. Funny Man. Well this isn't funny!"

"I don't think this is funny. I already told you that I didn't even know you were still here."

"Well, leave it to you to not know! Everybody else in town knows that I am over here!"

141

"Is everything okay here?" Kate asked from behind Mia.

"No. Everything is certainly not all right. I cannot believe Cooper is the contractor you were talking about. And he's the one that you think is hot? Seriously?"

"Mia," she whispered. "Way to keep a secret!"

"I don't care about keeping secrets. Did he even tell you who he is?"

She looked over at Cooper and then back at Mia, confusion on her face. "No. I don't understand what's happening here."

"I'll tell you what, I'll leave you two alone so he can explain exactly who he is. And then I want him off my property and out of my life."

Mia turned and walked back in the house, went up the stairs and slammed the door to her bedroom.

CHAPTER 11

*K*ate stood there, staring at Cooper as he leaned over, his elbows on his knees, running his fingers through his hair.

"Are you going to answer me?" she asked, as they sat on the front porch.

"Look, I'm really sorry about all of this. I didn't know you were Mia's sister."

"Well, I didn't know that until recently either. What's going on? How do you and Mia know each other?"

"I've known Mia since she moved here. We met when we started middle school."

"Then what in the world is going on? Why does she hate you so much?"

"I was kind of… a jerk… back then."

"What does that even mean, Cooper?"

He groaned, as if he didn't want the words to come out of his mouth. "I guess you would've referred to me as a… bully."

"Oh no," Kate said.

"Yeah. I picked on her a lot because of her height and her squeaky little voice."

"Why would you do that?" Kate asked, standing up.

"Because I was an idiot teenage boy who thought he was cool. I feel horrible about it now."

"Then why haven't you apologized?"

He stood. "Kate, I've tried. Really, I have. Every time I saw Mia around town, I'd try to talk to her. She wouldn't listen at all, and then I left a few years ago for work."

"You need to leave."

"You're probably right," he said, standing up. "Before I leave, I want you to know that I think you're really nice, and I'd still love to have that dinner by the river with you. But I understand if you can't do that."

"Listen, I just met Mia myself, but she's my sister. And I feel a strong connection to her and to this place. There's no way I'm going to screw that up over any man. I hope you can appreciate that."

He nodded his head. "I respect that." He started to walk away, turning back one last time. "If you still need my help with this property, I'm just a phone call away."

She laughed under her breath before turning to walk in the house.

~

Mia stood at the kitchen sink, her hands gripping the counter until they were red. Something about seeing Cooper again after all these years made rage well up within her.

"Hey." She turned around to see Kate standing there. She didn't know how to feel. Anger? Resentment?

"Hey."

Kate walked closer and then sat down on one of the stools at the breakfast bar. "I had no idea you knew Cooper."

"Oh yes, I definitely know Cooper."

"Can you tell me what happened?"

"What did he tell you?"

"That he was an idiot and bullied you."

Mia laughed. "Oh, is that all he told you? Typical Cooper."

"I feel like I'm completely in the dark here. Can you tell me what's going on?"

Mia sighed and sat down on the other stool. "Cooper was the ringleader of a very bad four years of my life. He and his cronies taunted me to no end, making up nicknames and just generally making my life miserable. I cried every single day after school."

"Oh my gosh, Mia. I'm so sorry. I would never have brought him here..."

"I guess I should get over it. I'm thirty-four years old, after all. But when I saw him standing there, I just lost it. I was taken straight back to those days."

"Has he tried to apologize?"

"He has a few times over the years, but I just walked away. I didn't want to hear it."

"I had no idea. If I had even known there was a possibility you knew him…"

Mia put up her hand. "It's okay. I know you didn't know, and honestly maybe I should give him a chance. We've all grown up a lot since then, but it just all came rushing back when I saw him."

"Well, as far as I'm concerned, you don't ever have to see him again."

Mia smiled. "What are the odds that the guy you have the hots for would be my high school bully?"

Kate laughed. "Well, in a town this size, I'd say the odds are pretty good. There's not exactly a hot singles scene here, is there?"

"You really like him?"

Kate shrugged. "Not as much as I thought I did. I mean, at first he came off as cocky and kind of abrasive. But when I went to look at his work, I saw a whole different side of him. I think he puts up some kind of wall, but I'm no psychologist."

Mia nodded. "As I got older, I often wondered whether something was going on at home that was causing him to act that way. But, when you're the one being bullied, you don't really care what's going on at the bully's house."

"Well, for right now, we need to figure out who we can get to come out here and do this work. Maybe we could call in some contractors from a little further away."

Mia sucked in a deep breath and blew it out

slowly. "We don't have time for that. If we don't get on this, like tomorrow, we are going to lose this wedding. Maybe…"

"Maybe what?"

"Maybe Cooper could come back out and give us an estimate. If you say his work is good…"

"Are you crazy? I don't want him around here if it's going to upset you."

"It was just a surprise, that's all. I should have taken a deep breath before kicking him off my property. Let's have him come give an estimate."

"Are you sure? Because I will stay on my phone all night calling other contractors…"

Mia laughed. "I know. And I appreciate that. But this is something I think I need to confront, and honestly, we need the work done as quickly as possible. Having somebody local is the best way to go."

"Okay. I'll text him and see if he can come back over this afternoon. Will that work?"

"Yes. Time to try to work this out since he has moved back to town. I just hope he's changed."

"Me too."

~

COOPER STOOD THERE, his hands in his pockets. He hadn't even walked up the stairs yet. He was just standing there, like he wasn't sure exactly what to do, kicking gravel around with his boot.

Mia stood at the top of the stairs on the porch,

staring down at him. It was probably the only time in her life she would ever be taller than Cooper.

"I'm surprised you called me back out here," he said.

"Me too. But the reality is that we need this work done quickly and we need it to look good, And Kate seems to be confident in your craftsmanship," Mia said, not making eye contact. Kate had stayed inside, opting instead to let Mia and Cooper have some time alone to talk.

"Mia, I want to tell you how incredibly sorry I am for how I acted when we were in high school. That was a really difficult time in my life for several reasons, but it didn't give me the right to take it out on you."

"I appreciate you saying that."

He looked up at her, and she found it remarkable how he actually did look sorry. It wasn't the same face she had remembered from high school; it was more weathered now with some wrinkles around the eyes. But he actually looked like a genuine person.

"No, really, I want you to understand that I have felt bad about this for so many years. I just had some things happening at home, and it made me really angry. And that anger spilled into school. It gave me a way to distract myself. I don't know what to do to make amends to you other than telling you that I'm going to build these structures for free."

Mia's mouth dropped open. "No, you're not. We're paying you."

"Look, I need something that will make me feel like I've made amends with you. It's the one part of my history that I can't ever seem to get over. Let me do this. Let me gift this to you and to this B&B so that I know I've done everything I could to make it up to you."

"Cooper, this is ridiculous. It's going to be a ton of work. You don't even know what we need yet," she said, throwing her hands up in the air.

He smiled. "It doesn't matter what you need. I will get it done, in a timely manner, and then maybe you can actually look at me without wanting to scream or cry or punch me in the nose."

Her anger melted away slightly, like an iceberg that was starting to sink into the ocean and break apart. "Thank you. I don't know what to say."

"Just say that you'll keep an open mind and let me show you how much I've changed."

She cocked her head to the side, squinting her eyes. "Are you doing this because you have a crush on my sister?"

He chuckled. "No. I would be doing this whether I had met Kate or not. Although, I hope by the end of this, you might let me take her out on a date."

Mia rolled her eyes. "We'll see. I'm not making any promises."

"Fair enough. So, why don't you show me what you guys are thinking."

KATE STOOD out in the middle of the backyard, looking in every direction, trying her best to figure out the right plan for the wedding. She had planned many receptions and parties, but a wedding was a whole different animal.

She and Mia had spent a lot of time the day before sketching everything out. Cooper had taken that and drawn even more ideas until they had a magnificent plan. Still, she worried that they were missing something.

"You okay?" Cooper asked, a lazy smile on his face.

"Yeah. Just wanna make sure we've covered everything."

He laughed. "Trust me, there's not much else we can fit back here if you keep adding projects."

"So, what are you working on now?"

"I figured the dance floor would be the easiest thing to do first. I've already got the frame, so it's just a matter of getting everything put together. I'm going to put a stain and seal on it so that it lasts a good long while. It will have some hinges that will make it easier for us to get it out-of-the-way when there's not an event going on back here."

"Good. And the gazebo?"

"I'm going to start on that in a couple of days. We should have everything done in plenty of time for your guests to come check it out."

Kate and Mia had decided not to tell Cooper about the big secret. He knew there was a wedding taking place, but he had no idea it was for a celebrity.

The less people that knew, the better. They didn't want word to get out and lose the opportunity and the money that was going to come from it.

"Good. Well, I'll leave you to it."

She turned and started walking toward the house. "Hey, Kate?"

"Yeah?" She said, turning around, her arms crossed. She still had hard feelings every time she thought about him bullying her sister all those years ago.

"I know we've gotten off on the wrong foot a couple of times now. I just want to say that I'm sorry about everything."

"You don't have to apologize to me. I'm just here to make sure this job gets done for my sister."

"I know. I'll get back to work," he said, a sad sort of look on his face.

As she walked back toward the house, all she could think about was turning around and running straight into his arms like some kind of romance novel. But thankfully her logical mind prevailed. Nothing good could come from falling in love with Cooper.

~

As Kate helped Mia wash the evening dishes, the new guests went upstairs to retire for the night. Dinner had been pot roast and mashed potatoes, and Kate was getting very accustomed to southern food.

Evie hadn't come down for dinner, texting she

was still too full from lunch and was going to watch some videos in their room.

"Maybe I should go up and make sure that she doesn't want something to eat before we put all of this away," Kate said. She glanced out the window into the backyard and saw Cooper still working away even though the sun was going down.

"Okay. Just let me know if she wants me to make her a plate. Do you think he's going to go home soon?" Mia said, laughing.

"Who knows? He's on quite a guilt trip, so we might even get a new wing built on this place before it's over with," Kate said, laughing as she ran up the stairs.

She walked down the hall and into her room, but Evie wasn't there. She checked the bathroom and every other room down the hallway that she could. No sign of her. She ran back down the stairs and looked around the living room.

"What's wrong?"

"It's Evie. She wasn't in the room. I didn't see her leave, did you?"

"No. I thought she was up there this whole time. She must've slipped out while we were talking to the guests," Mia said, wiping her hands on a dish towel and walking into the living room. "She couldn't have gone far. Maybe she just went out to sit by the lake or something."

Kate and Mia walked out the front door and started looking around the property. They walked down to the lake, back to where Cooper was working and all the way around the other side. There was no sign of her.

Kate was starting to get really nervous. It was almost dark, so she pulled out her phone and called Evie's. It went straight to voicemail. "Oh no, her phone must be dead. What should we do?"

"Everything okay?" Cooper asked, as he walked up.

"Kate's daughter is missing. Have you seen her?"

"No, sorry. I was back here hammering away. I didn't see anyone, not for the last few hours."

Kate started to shake. "Oh my gosh. Oh my gosh."

"Take some deep breaths, Kate. I'm sure she's fine. She'll probably be back in a few minutes. She couldn't have gone far, especially not without a car."

"Why would she do this? Why would she just wander off?"

"You know she likes to go explore. Why don't we get the golf cart and drive around a little bit and see if we can find her."

"I'll drive," Cooper said. Both women looked at him for a moment and then everybody turned and headed towards the golf cart.

~

MIA HAD NEVER FELT SO helpless in her life. They rode around the property, calling Evie's name over and over, to no avail. It was like she had vanished into thin air.

Finally, as the hours wore on, they called the

police. Unfortunately, Carter's Hollow was a tiny town with only a couple of deputies. They were handling a car accident on the edge of town, so they wouldn't be available to search for her until daylight.

That left it up to Kate, Cooper and Mia to try to find her, and they were having absolutely no luck. It was almost midnight, and she still wasn't back. Mia had a terrible feeling in the pit of her stomach.

At least it was June which meant it wasn't cold at night. But not knowing where her niece was with so much rocky terrain and possibly dangerous animals made her feel sick to her stomach. For some reason, she felt guilty, even though she hadn't done a thing. She just wanted to find Evie and bring her back home safely.

"Why don't I put on a pot of coffee?" Cooper said as they sat in the living room. There was nowhere else to look, and Kate's voice was hoarse from screaming her daughter's name for so many hours.

"That would be great. Thanks, Cooper," Mia said. Those were words that she never thought she'd hear come out of her mouth.

"I just don't understand this. Evie has always been a spontaneous kid, but she's never just left like this without telling me. I'm so scared," Kate said. Mia put her arm around her sister and pulled her close.

"We're going to find her. Everything is going to be okay. We just need daylight to come." Even as she said it, she didn't know if she was right. Was she giving her sister false hope?

"She could get eaten by a bear or bitten by a

snake before then. I have to find her," Kate said, standing up and moving toward the door again, her voice almost a whisper now.

Cooper jogged over from the kitchen and stood in front of the door. "Kate, you're exhausted. Going back out there isn't going to help find her. I've grown up around these woods, and she's going to be fine. We used to camp out in this area all the time."

"I just can't do this…" she said, bursting into tears. Cooper put his arms around her as she sobbed on his chest.

"We'll find her, Kate. I promise you."

Mia sat quietly, watching them. They really did seem to have some kind of a connection. She herself could never imagine dating Cooper, but that was because she had known him as a very immature adolescent boy. Standing before her was a man, and he was doing a great job at comforting her sister.

"I think I'm going to send some texts and emails to the neighbors I know around here. Maybe somebody has seen her," Mia said, standing up and walking over to her laptop.

"If anything happens to her, I will never forgive myself," Kate said.

"Kate, trust me. I know you don't have any real reason to, but we will get her back safely," Cooper said.

This was going to be the longest night of Kate and Mia's life.

CHAPTER 12

*E*xhaustion is a funny thing. No matter how stressed out a person is, eventually the body takes over and shuts down. And that's exactly what happened to Kate. Against everything she had in her, her body fell asleep.

When her eyes flickered open, sunlight was streaming through the window. She jumped to her feet, her eyes are still blurry from sleep.

"We have to get out there and find her!" she yelled. Mia, who was asleep on the sofa, bolted upright.

"Is she back? Did she come back?"

They both looked around in confusion. "Where's Cooper?"

"I don't know. But we have to get out there and find her," Kate said. She slipped on her sneakers as quickly as possible and ran to the front door, flinging it open. As they both ran out onto the porch, they saw the most beautiful sight. Cooper was carrying Evie down the driveway.

Kate ran towards them, concerned that Evie was hurt.

"Oh my gosh! Is she okay? Are you okay, Evie?" she yelled, her voice still strained from the night before.

Cooper smiled. "She's fine. She just had a little bit of an adventure."

"I'm alright, Mom," Evie finally said, her annoyed teenager tone coming out very clearly.

"Where were you?" Kate asked as Cooper slowly put her down. Evie was favoring her right ankle, holding it in the air slightly.

"There's this creek down the ravine that I have always wanted to get to. I had been going over there a lot lately, trying to figure out a path. Last night, I thought I had figured it out so I decided to run over there before the sun went down and see if I could get to the creek. I ended up slipping and falling. I think I sprained my ankle."

"Evie! You had us all scared to death. We even called the police! Don't you ever do something like that again!" Kate said, her emotions getting the better of her.

"I know, Mom. I'm so sorry I worried everybody. When I went, I didn't know my phone was almost dead. And Cooper said you guys were yelling for me, but I couldn't hear a thing down there. It was pretty scary staying down there all night."

Kate reached out and pulled her daughter into a

tight embrace. "I'm just so grateful that you're alive. I don't know what I would've done…"

"Let's not think about that. Why don't we get you into the house. I'm sure you're starving," Mia said.

"Yeah, I'm hungry, and I'd like to get off of my ankle for awhile."

"I'll take you in the house and get you an ice pack for that ankle," Mia said. Evie leaned on her aunt as they walked up the steps and into the house.

"She'll be okay," Cooper said. "Just make sure she elevates that ankle as much as possible today. I hurt mine a few years ago and…"

"Thank you."

He smiled. "You're most welcome, Kate."

"How did you find her?"

"I went out as soon as it was daybreak. And then I started thinking about all of the places around here that I would've been exploring at her age. I remembered the creek, so I decided to check it out."

Without thinking, Kate ran forward and hugged him tightly. He stood there for a moment, his arms hanging by his side, and then pulled her into an embrace. She couldn't deny that it felt right to be standing in his arms.

Finally, she stepped back. "I'm sorry I've been so tough on you."

He smiled. "Let's just call it even."

"I better get inside. I want to soak up as much time as possible with my daughter."

She turned and started walking back toward the house. "Hey, Kate?"

"Yeah?"

"Does saving your daughter qualify me to ask you on an official date?"

She smiled. "Let's just see how well you do on those construction projects first."

She could feel him watching her as she walked back in the house, but she really didn't mind that at all.

*M*ia couldn't remember a time when she had been more nervous. As they all stood outside on the porch, including Cooper, waiting for Lana Blaze and her wedding party to arrive, she felt the weight of the world on her shoulders.

If this whole thing fell apart or if the news media suddenly showed up, they wouldn't get their bonus, and they'd have a terrible reputation for any future celebrity guests who might want to come.

"Where are they? You know if they're driving in limousines, everybody in town's going to know something's happening," Mia said.

Evie laughed. "Oh, Aunt Mia, they aren't going to drive here in limousines. They'll probably be in SUVs or something like that."

"I'm sure this isn't their first rodeo," Cooper said. "I just hope they like everything I built out there."

Kate smiled. "I'm sure they're going to love it.

That gazebo is beyond anything I could've imagined. The detail work you did on that is amazing."

As Mia watched her sister and Cooper smile at each other, she felt happy for them. Over the last few weeks of working together, she and Cooper had forged a friendship, and she had forgiven him for all of those times he made her feel bad in high school.

Although he hadn't really opened up about whatever happened at his home when he was a kid to make him act that way, she didn't need to know. She knew he was sorry, and on top of that he had managed to build a beautiful wedding venue for free and save her niece. She figured they were even.

"Is that them? I think I see a car," Kate said, looking up the road.

Several vehicles pulled in one right after another. Mia felt like she was going to throw up. Not only was she was about to meet one of the biggest celebrities in the world, but she had to entertain and feed an entire wedding party full of other celebrities and their friends and family. This was going to be a very memorable day.

A black SUV stopped right in front of the porch, and a woman stepped out wearing a business suit.

"Are you Mia?" she asked.

"Yes, that's me."

"Hi. I am Nancy Goddard, Lana's personal assistant. Nice to meet you."

"Nice to meet you too."

"Are you ready for us?"

"Of course. Please come inside. We can show all

of you to your rooms and show Lana the special space we have created for her to get ready for her big day!"

As everyone got out of the vehicles and started heading inside, Kate and Mia waited for Lana to step out of the vehicle. A few moments later, she did.

She was even more beautiful in person. She smiled, looking radiant as any bride would on her wedding day.

"Hi! Thank you so much for allowing me to have my wedding here. I have such fond memories of visiting when I was a kid," Lana said, shaking everyone's hand.

"It's an honor to have you here. I don't remember when you stayed, but I was probably pretty young myself," Mia said, smiling.

"I remember your mother, and I was so sad to hear that she had passed away. She made the most amazing food. I'm looking forward to having that for my guests."

"We've cooked up plenty for your celebration. I hope you enjoy it."

As she walked into the house, leaving Mia, Kate, Evie and Cooper standing on the front porch, they all let out a collective breath.

"I guess it's showtime," Kate said.

"Yeah, and hopefully I don't throw up," Mia said, rubbing her stomach.

~

THE WEDDING HAD GONE off without a hitch, and they got paid their big bonus. Never had Kate been so relieved about anything in her life.

Of course, it was almost time for her and her daughter to go home, but she was second guessing that. She was starting to fall in love with the B&B, the little town and, quite possibly, Cooper.

Although they hadn't gone out on that official date yet, she felt her self growing closer to him. But now she had to make the decision about whether to go back to her life in Rhode Island and continue building her business or stay at the B&B and start a brand new life.

"Is anyone else as exhausted as I am?" Mia asked as she laid her head back against the chair.

"I just can't believe that I got to meet Lana Blaze! We took so many pictures. Her people said that I can post them after the People magazine article comes out next week," Evie said, scrolling through the photos on her phone.

"I'm glad all of my carpentry held up. They had so many people on the dance floor at one point that I was afraid the whole thing might fall through," Cooper said, laughing.

"You really shouldn't tell people that," Kate said, rolling her eyes.

"I guess I better check my email. I haven't done that in a few days, so I don't know if we have any new guests arriving soon."

"Mom, we're not going back to Rhode Island, are we?" Evie suddenly asked.

Kate didn't know what to say. She hated when her daughter put her on the spot. "Evie, can we talk about this later?"

"I'd kind of like to know the answer to that myself," Cooper said.

"Me too," Mia said from across the room.

Kate paused for a long moment. "I still can't make any long-term promises," she said. She didn't know why she couldn't promise to stay the full six months, but right now she was still undecided. Something was still nagging at her about leaving behind her life in Rhode Island, and she didn't know what it was. It wasn't exactly like she had a boyfriend there or family.

Maybe it was just her independence. Maybe it was that part of her that was used to not having any family to answer or to depend on.

"But," she said. "I think we will stay for at least a bit longer. I'd like to help you get some more wedding business coming in at the very least."

Mia smiled. "Good. I've got a lot more to teach you about being Southern."

Evie leaned over and hugged her mom. "Thank you. I wasn't ready to leave this place. It feels like home."

With that, she ran upstairs. It made Kate feel good that her daughter felt at home.

"Does this mean we can go on our date now?" Cooper asked.

"You're just not going to give up, are you?"

"Never," he said, winking at her.

"Oh my gosh…" Mia said from the computer.

"What's the matter?"

Mia sat there, silently staring at the computer screen for a few moments. Then she looked at Kate.

"I just got another match on the DNA site."

$$\sim$$

VISIT WWW.RACHELHANNAAUTHOR.COM TO see all of Rachel's books and book 2 in this series!

Made in the USA
Monee, IL
18 March 2022

93117056R10100